It's Been Bertalised

(or how a Gordon Setter ruined my life)
And other true short stories

David Rex Harkness

authorHOUSE®

AuthorHouse™ UK Ltd.
500 Avebury Boulevard
Central Milton Keynes, MK9 2BE
www.authorhouse.co.uk
Phone: 08001974150

© 2009 David Rex Harkness. All rights reserved.

No part of this book may be reproduced, stored in a retrieval system, or transmitted by any means without the written permission of the author.

First published by AuthorHouse 12/18/2009

ISBN: 978-1-4490-6252-1 (sc)

This book is printed on acid-free paper.

"It's Been Bertalised"

A collection of true, amusing, short stories from the life of the author. The collection encompasses a number of tales relating both to several animals we have owned, and to various amusing incidents, involving people who's company I have enjoyed, over a 40 year period.

This book is dedicated to my wife 'Dottie',
who had a constant love/hate relationship with 'Bertie'.

'Bertie'

Contents

Introduction		**xi**
Part 1	**Animal friends.**	**1**
Tale 1	"It's been Bertalised"	1
Tale 2	Freddie	17
Tale 3	'The Big Game Hunter'	21
Tale 4	The Tale of Lusso's Tail.	24
Part 2	**A lesser kind of animal. 'Man'**	**29**
Tale 5	"The Welcome Inn"	30
Tale 6	"A Visit to HMS Sheffield"	33
Tale 7	'A visit to HMS Campbeltown'	38
Tale 8	Denzil by name	42
Tale 9	A Visit to the British Embassy in Bern	46
Tale 10	Lord Winestock visits Eastwood House.	50
Tale 11	The 'Big Robbery'	52
Tale 12	Guides and Markers.	54
Tale 13	A Weekend in Beirut	57
Tale 14	Burglar Alarms	60
Tale 15	A visit to HMS London	64
Tale 16	Lord Harkness of Kilnsea	69
Tale 17	Being driven to drink	72
Tale 18	Highly Confidential	74
Tale 19	'Working for a living'	76
Tale 20	The Big Hard Farmer.	79
Tale 21	"Mike and the Casino girl"	80
Tale 22	"Under cover in Switzerland"	83
Tale 23	"The Disco"	85
Tale 24	"A new cocktail"	87
'And Finally'	"A bit more on Freddie and his friends."	89

Introduction

My wife Dottie and I had just moved from a small cottage in the Pembrokeshire National park to a run down old farmhouse with 2.5 acres in Galloway, Scotland. Along with us came a very friendly and intelligent 7 year of age "Old English" sheepdog called George and a cat by the name of "Fluffy."

George was everybody's friend, and just tended to roam freely around the adjoining farm land and buildings and although he was generally a scruff pot he had never in his lifetime done a single item of damage, that I can remember. George possessed a large cardboard box filled with balls of various sorts and colours. (I normally bought him a new one every Friday when I came home from working in the Lake district.) His big trick was to be able to individually identify each ball after only a short period of possession. If you said "George fetch the Red spotted ball" he would search through the box until he identified the correct one then dig it out and bring it to you.

Life generally was pretty good, Dottie had moved close to her son and family and I had a project for life trying to turn a sows ear of a house into a silk purse. The house had been rented prior to my purchase and very little had been done to maintain the property over the previous 50 years. Rain had been coming in constantly and some of the main beams were hanging down in the kitchen area so this was going to be my hobby for the next 10 years along with a full time job elsewhere in the country. The first thing that happened was to lose the cat under the floorboards. She was subsequently recovered unharmed and work progressed well. Dottie project managed all the modifications, design requirements and assorted task allocations from the comfort of her armchair while I multiplexed as demolition engineer, builder, decorator and general dogs body.

Sadly after only around a year from moving in, George stopped eating and was generally not the happy fit dog he had always been. We rushed him into Stranraer to the local vets who subsequently found him to have a major untreatable growth in his stomach. (Possibly caused by eating poisoned rat bait put down by the local farmer.) On the advice of the vet we agreed to have him put to sleep and even I, who never cried at anything but old movies shed a tear or two. We have had a number of greatly loved dogs but none we have missed so badly.

For the first month after loosing George we did nothing, but then the subject of a replacement started to enter the conversation. We considered St. Bernard's of which we had previously owned 4, however these had all died at an early age when you are just getting to know them well. Several other breeds were on the short list;

Pyrenean, Newfoundland, King Charles etc. when we noticed an advert for Gordon setter pups in Dumfries only 75 miles away. My wife said a setter was not a good idea as they were notoriously daft and lacking in brains. However a local Scots girl (who will remain anonymous) assured us that Gordon setters were not like other setters! "What she failed to indicate was that they are far far worse."

So we rang the breeder who still had 3 pups and agreed to drive over that weekend.

In preparation for the arrival of the new 8week old pup I spent around 2 days boarding up the bottom 3 feet of the downstairs shower room in order to give the pup somewhere pleasant and warm to live. After surveying my handiwork, I lovingly placed a blanket on the floor along with a selection of toys and a water bowl. How could the pup not be happy?

So the next day Dottie and I set off on the 75mile drive to Dumfries to look at the puppies. These turned out to be on a farm on the border of a wildlife nature reserve. The young couple who had bred the dogs introduced us to the mother who appeared very gentle and docile, we then went on to look at the pups who were languishing inside a barn.

I immediately selected the biggest and friendliest of the pups who were 10 weeks old and after a longish chat to the owners, Dottie, I and 'Bertie' headed off home. Well all I can say is that he was good as gold on the 2 hour journey back. "We've got a good one here" I said to Dottie. (How naive is it possible to be.?) .

Everything went well until bed time. The puppy had been fed and watered and I shut it into my modified shower room in preparation for a good nights sleep. No sooner had the door shut than the most horrifying and disturbing weeping and wailing started up! I didn't believe a 10 week old puppy could generate so much noise. However I said to Dottie "ignore it and it will soon settle down". Off to bed we went but sleep was impossible the noise went on and on and on. So around 2am the puppy won and was carried upstairs to sleep next to Dotties bed. He only settled down when actualy allowed to sleep on the bed which was a bit odd for a pup that had been brought up in a barn. Perfect peace for the rest of the night. This should also have been a guide to the future as we subsequently learnt that Gordon Setters go into a mindless panic whenever they are left alone.

From there on life started to get tough. Much as we loved him and in his way he was a very lovable dog he immediately started to destroy our house, belongings car and peace of mind.

The following is a record as best I remember, of life with Bertie and I am sure I have forgotten to include many a misdeed!

CHAPTER 1

CHAOS AND WRECKAGE

Well the puppy started off in much the same way as many puppies do, peeing everywhere 'but' outside and chewing a few minor items like the odd chair leg and a mobile phone. He had a great sense of fun and treated the bedroom stairs as a playground even though he didn't know how to descend properly. He would get up OK but then the downward trip became quite entertaining sometimes forwards, sometimes backwards but invariably either on his tummy or just rolling end over end until he came up against the wall at the bottom.

It was only then we realised he had a very bad habit. Nothing tasted better to him than his own turds (or stools if you are posh) and these were at their best when still hot. After around 2 months of this he began to realise that we were not too keen on his habit after being reprimanded continually (we think life had probably been a bit tough before we acquired him and his droppings had become a food supplement). So he changed his ways by becoming more devious. He would plop-a-dop (The wife's term for doing his business) and then look round to see if you were watching him and if he thought not then down it would go. If he could see you looking at him he would casually wander away only to return and complete the terrible deed when the coast was clear. Needless to say his breath was appalling, so we consulted the vet. First we tried some liquid chemical purchased at great expense only to find it made not a blind bit of difference. Then we were told by one of the vets that if we added a bit of pineapple to his food he wouldn't like the taste, so we bought several tins of pineapple only to find that this also did not deter him. We were then told it was because the pineapple was not fresh and we then bought fresh pineapple. "Not a jot of difference". It was around 3 years before he stopped eating his droppings and I still suspect on a dark night he was still occasionally having a late night snack right up to the day he died (Which oddly enough was from a stomach tumour!)

When he was about 4 months old I started to take him for short journeys in my car. At the time I was using a 6 year old Volvo estate which was ideal for the dogs and although it couldn't be described as showroom the vehicle was in pretty good nick. The back was dedicated to dogs with a standard dog guard at the rear of the back seats. After several short journeys that he appeared to enjoy I drove into the nearest town of Stranraer about 7 miles away and parked in Morrisons supermarket. Now the big mistake! I popped into the supermarket to get some item, probably a bottle of whisky and could not have been gone more than 10 minutes only to find on my return that 'Bertie' had been in total panic at being left alone and was trying desperately to chew his way out of the car. He had managed to generate a decent sized hole in the dog guard and was unhappily dismantling the back seats and head cloth in an effort to get out. However it is fair to say that he had a comfortable trip home surrounded by lots of newly generated dog bedding. (I subsequently got £150 for the Volvo).

Things seemed to be going moderately well for a while and knowing Bertie didn't like the car we went off to do the weekly shop, leaving the dog the run of the house. I suppose we were away for around 2 hours and upon our return as we approached the house it became apparent all was not well. "Have you taken the Dining room curtains down for washing" I said "Not likely" was the reply. Well on entering we were surrounded by total chaos! The passageway pot board had a nicely modified leg, the wood chippings from this were neatly mixed up with quantities of what looked like confetti but had been the days mail of which none could be identified. Subsequently we had to be present whenever the post arrived or Bertie demolished it before we got there. As a result of this I kept getting threatening red letters for the following year or so as I didn't always pay my bills on time due to the mobile shredder having got there first.

Now into the Dining room. What fun had been had. Not only were the curtains and rod down but these had been improved by the odd chew. The dining chairs were all upended but basically still usable along with several pot plants now spread neatly over the floor. However Bertie was pleased to see us, so what can you do.

Next time we went out we took precautions, shutting the Dining and Sitting room doors before leaving. We also left Bertie with a handful of dog biscuits, to keep him occupied.

Upon returning we opened the door with trepidation expecting the worst, only to find Bertie lying just inside the door and no sign of any damage. I gave him a great big pat and told him what a good boy he had been. Things were improving (or so I thought). We settled down to a very pleasant lunch and half a bottle of wine and a couple of whisky's later I headed upstairs to change. (Yep you've got it!) Half way up the stairs I met the first remnants of what had been the bedroom chair, the cushion of which had been filled with a sort of fluffy stuffing which was now everywhere along with the bedding and several ornaments.

Over the next 18 months we estimated that Bertie cost us between 3 and 5 thousand pounds in various forms of damage.

Chapter 2

Neurosis.

Bertie had very expressive big brown eyes that somehow made you feel sorry for him, even when he was being at his worst. However behind those eyes there didn't appear to be much grey matter other than a large capacity to collect and develop a large number of neurosis. He had a very good pedigree with lots of champions in his recent ancestry and he was also undoubtedly, suffering from years of over interbreeding. He must have been about 4 months old when we decided that the answer to the problem was to get him another puppy as a companion.

Luckily a girl in Stranraer whose boyfriend was staying in a cottage not far from us, had recently had a litter of pups to a Labrador by some unknown wandering randy mongrel who is still somewhat unidentified but could have a lot of greyhound in him judging by the offspring's shape and athletic ability. However I digress! We chatted to Steve the boyfriend and he said he would discuss the sale of a puppy with his girlfriend that evening. Next thing we hear is a telephone call from the girl to say we could have the puppy that was presently with her boyfriend, for the sum of £100. I think the puppy was 3 months old, so not a lot younger than Bertie.

The next day we visited Steve and found the pup to be just what we wanted. Steve chatted with us about the puppy, and seemed very happy to see it go, to what should be a good home.

We then spent an entire day making the puppy feel at home and introducing it to Bertie who was immediately friendly towards it. By 8pm the household was calm the pup had eaten and was settled down for the first time since his arrival. Suddenly the doorbell rang 'a fairly unusual occurrence at that time, as we live way out in the country.'

. This turned out to be Sandra, 'Steve's girlfriend who was very apologetic and was cradling a golden puppy in her arms. "I'm awfully sorry" she said "but would you be willing to take this puppy, and let me have the other one back." It transpired that Steve had broken down shortly after we left and spent the rest of the day in tears crying for the loss of his pet. So we handed over our newly acquired pup and accepted his brother, who Sandra, had been keeping for herself, she also kindly left us his bed and a selection of toys he had been used to. (I thought I was soft with animals but after this I felt quite tough!)

So by now it was 9pm and we had to start again settling down another pup and get set for another sleepless night.

The pup had already been named 'Lusso' before we got him (apparently he was named after a brand of Italian spaghetti sauce! And I have since found that 'Lusso' means luxury in Italian.) However he turned out to be a good friendly and easily trained dog who would have been perfect had he not subsequently been taught a number of misdeeds by Bertie.

Adjacent to our garden (This is really just a field that I keep cut and have built a pond in) is a very large field that the local farmer uses constantly for young beasts or in winter to graze sheep from the hill farms. When the dogs were about 8 months old and beginning to feel confident and brave, the field was filled with a large number of sheep and these became very tempting. The dogs and in particular Bertie would run up and down the edge of the fence barking at the sheep and causing general panic. The faster the sheep ran the greater the fun. As the fence is only about 4 feet high it was only going to be a matter of time before one of the dogs jumped over or managed to squeeze under the fence and the consequences of this were not even to be contemplated. Bertie for all the fact that he appeared totally uncoordinated, could squeeze or dig his way under any fence.

I decided that for the dogs own good, we needed to put up an electric fence and so bought one of the less powerful models which gave out 8000volts but could do no lasting harm. I then spent several days erecting the fence on short stakes all round the field (sorry garden). The fence was approximately 1 foot off the ground and a source of intense interest to both dogs as they had watched me erect it. So I switched it on and stood back to observe the outcome. Firstly the fence was touched by Lusso who let out a yelp, and ran for home. As far as I remember that was all he needed to learn to stay clear in future but not so the dog member of 'Mensa' Bertie, who managed to get several shocks over the next few days culminating in 2 particular events.

I was doing something in the garden when I heard the most blood curdling squeals from behind me and upon turning round found that Bertie had tried to squeeze under the electric fence and got stuck half way through. Needless to say the fence was delivering a nice new shock every second or so and these were accompanied on each occasion with another yelp. I managed to rescue him fairly quickly by using the spade to lift the wire, but was he grateful, definitely not as he shot in the house not to emerge again that day. He remained stuffed in the corner and sulked, obviously blaming me for all his ills.

The second event was a week or two later. After the trauma of the fence incident he appeared to have learnt his lesson and did not touch the fence again. It was a lovely day sunny and warm with just a light breeze so I sat outside, armed with my Panama hat to ward off the sun, and a bottle of wine to ease relaxation. In this somewhat soporific state I spotted Bertie wandering aimlessly by the electric fence only to suddenly raise his leg and start 'peeing', the jet came out absolutely perfectly, to spray the electric fence. The noise made any previous squeals seem like a whisper as once again he shot in the house never to emerge. It's just as well we didn't intend to breed from him as his reproduction capability was probably seriously impaired.

We live in what is probably close to being the windiest and wettest place in Britain. The house is situated on top of a hill about quarter of a mile from a 100ft cliff face, looking directly out to the Irish sea. However on a calm clear day in summer it must be one of the nicest places to live in the world. On a clear day it is possible to see south beyond the Solway firth to the Cumbria coast, with the Isle of Man in the distance. To the west, both north and south Ireland can be clearly observed, Arran and the Mull of Kintyre to the north and to the east Luse bay and the Galloway hills. However for 4 months of the year we get howling winds and rain on such a regular basis that it would send most English southerners scampering off immediately to Spain, or somewhere equally unpleasant. Along with all this wind and rain there are a fair number of electric storms. Bertie was probably around 5 months old when the first clap of thunder arrived, and of cause this occurred in the middle of the night while Dottie was on her own. (I was working in Surrey at the time.)

Upon the arrival of the first flash of lightening and thunder, Bertie lost control of all his mental facilities and his physical ones went into overdrive. He knew that the 'Dog God' was trying to wreak vengeance upon him and shook and whined continuously, while jumping around the bedroom in a manner likely to remove the eye of anyone he came into contact with. He would try and climb into bed with my wife, and hide behind her while still maintaining a high level of panic. This would go on continuously throughout the storm and nothing would calm him down. This state of affairs continued throughout his life and he became an expert in predicting an oncoming storm, looking out of the window and starting to get agitated, long before we detected a storm was coming. In the end Dottie either didn't go to bed, or got up, and sat around downstairs holding his paw. This was invariably by the light of an oil lamp or candles as the other regular occurrence we endured if we had a storm was that the electricity went off, and of coarse this added to Berties general panic. Throughout these momentous occasions Lusso slept like a top.

'Lusso' and 'Finley' the cat.

CHAPTER 3

LIFE IN GENERAL.

As well as Lusso we also possessed a cat 'Finley'. The cat was older and wiser than either of the dogs, and they looked upon it as a mortal enemy during the day. The cat was quite capable of seeing either of them off if need be, but usually spent its days being chased from pillar to post. They would often gang up on Finley and get him trapped in a corner 'great fun' until he got totally fed up, and lashed out at the dog nose within easiest reach. In spite of a number of scratches to their noses they never tired of harassing the cat.

However when evening came these major enemies became the best of friends, with Bertie lying with his head on Lusso and the cat tucked up between them. All relaxing in front of the open stove.

Around 400yds down the farm road from us are our nearest neighbours, who being a farming family keep hens and ducks. When Bertie was around a year old he was just beginning to wander away from 'Cairnhill' whenever he got the chance.

We hadn't noticed he was missing, on this particular occasion until a very irate farmer appeared on our doorstep. Apparently something resembling the battle of the Somme had just taken place with feathers and bits of duck and hen everywhere. It appeared to have been nearly as catastrophic as when the fox previously visited. So there we were once again eating humble pie. Meanwhile Bertie was full of himself as once again he failed to understand the difference between good and bad "except that generally bad is better.

The second Christmas we had Bertie we prepared to celebrate as usual. This involved a minimum of decorations other than the Christmas tree, which we arranged in the dinning room and always spent a long time decorating. This year the tree was around 7ft tall and we spent most of the day in both putting on quantities of lights, and vast numbers of baubles, the lower ones providing great fun for the cat to batter about. Other than massively overeating and drinking, we didn't really celebrate as both of us are atheists and believe only that you should treat everyone and everything as you yourself would wish to be treated. So once again there I am full of wine, and totally relaxed. ' I make it sound as though all I do is eat and drink which is anything but the truth as when I am away I spend my days keeping missile system radars running, and when at home I am either building, working in the garden, cutting grass, fixing everything that has been broken or destroyed while away or working on my old cars, or steam engines.' Even so we manage a glass or two to help relax each day, so it was while sitting around post lunch that Dottie said I haven't seen Bertie for a couple of hours, have you locked him out? So the search began firstly in the garden and then down the lane to see if he had escaped. No luck. Finally we start to search the house shouting for Bertie with no response. Eventually I look into the dining room and was confronted with the most amazing sight. The Christmas tree was lying flat on the floor, baubles and decorations everywhere and in the middle of all this mess, sitting perfectly still and tangled in a mass of flashing fairy lights, was a Gordon Setter totally still and looking extremely bemused. I wish I had taken a photo as words could not describe the expression on his face. All the time we had been searching and shouting for him, he never let on he was there! I like to think it was because his conscience was troubling him, but really know it was just because he's as daft as a brush.

This same trait would show in other ways such as if he was accidentally locked out of the front door he would sit quietly on the doorstep until rescued, never barking or letting on in other ways, no matter how long he was there. Oddly enough, if he was at the back door he would make a fuss to get in.

So after replacing my car with something we were not too ashamed of, I bought Bertie a muzzle. This was only for wearing in the car to prevent further damage, not to make him appear safe to strangers. In fact he was extremely friendly but had a bad habit of jumping up at total strangers, and scaring them rigid, he was big and heavy for a Gordon setter, about the same size as a small wolfhound but totally out of control of any of his limbs, so he wasn't always popular with strangers but he was fondly under the impression everyone adored him. Anyway equipped with his muzzle Bertie, Lusso and I would head for the beach each day. We live within easy walking distance of the beach, however it is necessary to negotiate a large cliff to get down, so instead we would drive 7miles each way to a rocky beach, that was seldom used by tourists. Bertie's muzzle was removed as soon as we arrived, and the moment both dogs were released they charged down to the sea. Lusso heading straight in to try and catch a seal or oystercatcher, and Bertie just to paddle in the shallows. Then they would be off after anything that moved, and at this point Bertie became stone deaf. Lusso would return on being called but not Bertie, who could usually detect another walker and their dog about half a mile away. Well by the time I managed to catch up once again, chaos rained, with most dog owners of pension able age, waving walking sticks, bellowing, and generally in a state of panic, and if their dog happened to be a bitch and in season you can imagine the rest. Bertie loved it all 'what fun'.

The beach was deserted for around a mile in each direction except for one little cottage close to the beach, and considering the wide choice he had, Bertie invariably considered directly outside the cottage door as the best place to do his business. This meant that although we had a rocky deserted beach as far as the eye could see I still had to collect his droppings and cart them home, especially as I could detect the cottage owner peering out from behind the curtains.

Back to the car and then the next nutty episode regularly took place. Bertie as a puppy had been lifted into the back of the car and now decided this was the correct way to get in. He would jump in and out several times and then stand there waiting to be lifted in. Unfortunately he passed this stupid idea on to Lusso, who even now waits to be lifted into the back of the car.

"WINE,WINE,WINE."

That's the sort you drink not the type wives are fond of.

Bertie was a consummate thief, and no amount of scolding made any difference to how he behaved. He would steal food off the kitchen bench, or even the dining table if he could get away with it. He even learnt how to open the kitchen peddle bin and steal the leftovers so we ended up placing a heavy weight on the top of the peddle bin, to prevent his access. This of course made the bin pretty awkward to use. As well as stealing food he would steal anything that he could lift and if it was small enough he would eat it otherwise it got buried.

Just a few of the things he ate were 2 of Lusso,s collars but left the metal bits, socks by the sack load and on one occasion, I remember a perfect sock coming out of his rear end totally encasing a nice big turd. He ate dusters, knickers, dog toys galore, in fact I stopped buying him dog toys as they only lasted about 2 minutes before they were consumed. Meanwhile he was still busily wrecking the house up to the age of three. This included an electric massage chair he had spotted a mouse vanishing underneath. He managed to rip most of the leather away, and expose most of the vital parts before we stopped him, meanwhile the mouse dived under the sideboard to live another day. The back door still shows the effects of a dog locked out for two minutes, and to this day has plywood nailed over the bottom half. Other items to be destroyed, consumed or buried include mobile phones, remote controls, library books, cookery books, gardening books, kitchen utensils, the stair carpet, dinning table legs, several cat doors by jamming his head through and he totally destroyed the garden stream and pond. Plus lots more but you get the idea. The term 'It's been Bertalised' is now part of our households general language. Even now 2 years after his death if anything is damaged we use the term 'it's been Bertalised'

However this has little to do with the wine. At weekends I enjoyed a long lunch, and Bertie and Lusso knew that as soon as lunch was over we would go walking in the fields, so they would impatiently wait for me to finish eating and drinking. As time went on Bertie became more and more of a pest, and started agitating to go out earlier and earlier. In order to combat this I would hold up my wine glass, point at the level of the wine and say "Wine". Bertie soon became an expert at judging how far down the glass I had got and as it neared the bottom he would jump up ready to go. Where this tended to go wrong is when I was only on the first glass, reached for the bottle to top up, and suddenly we had a full glass again. It was now necessary to raise the glass point at the level and say "Wine" again. Bertie would then lie down in a sulk until we approached the dregs again and the whole performance would be repeated until eventually lunch was concluded, and we went walkies.

In spite of being thick as two short planks and having no conscience, Bertie was surprisingly sensitive when in the wrong. If he was shouted at for some miss deed or other he would roll on his back in supplication and wet himself. This continued right up to the day he died, and as such he was able to use it as a form of defence as we avoided shouting at him in order to protect the carpets from too many stains.

Endgame!
When we acquired Bertie we were told it was impossible to train Gordon setters for at least a year so we initially looked forward to this date, only to find that the professional advice was wait 2 years at least. During this time Dottie spent her life saying how badly she hated him, and threatening to send him to a dogs home. However we felt he would soon improve and when 2 years had gone by we presumed he would be OK next year and so on right up to the age of 6. Of course he never did do as expected of a normal dog, and managed to teach Lusso lots of bad habits. Lusso otherwise was a great dog, easily trained and friendly to everyone.

One morning Bertie would not eat his food for the first time in his life and was generally not his usual happy self. I was away from home so Dottie got the vet out to look at him and while trying to examine him Bertie bit him, something he had never done before. He was taken into Stranraer, for examination and 2 hours later the vet telephoned and carefully explained that they had opened him up and he had a large inoperable tumour in his stomach, that had burst. The decision was made to put him to sleep.

Well for someone who had supposedly hated him all his life, Dottie spent the entire day in tears.

Even now we both still miss him a lot and will probably never have a dog with so much character ever again.

BE R TIE
I
P

"Freddie"

Once again we were looking for another puppy and 3 months after the loss of Bertie we decided on another Saint Bernard. We had previously had 4 of these but the last one was fifteen years previously.

So after perusing the press and internet we found a litter of puppies with a good pedigree over in Lincolnshire and I arranged to drive over and collect one the following Saturday.

As I lived in south west Scotland and at the time was working in Cumbria this involved around a 500mile journey from Barrow-in-Furness to Immingham Lincolnshire then back to Portpatrick in Scotland, 300 of these miles with the puppy in tow. I had a box in the car with bedding inside to keep the puppy happy.

I arrived at the breeders around 11-30am, a very pleasant young couple who introduced me to the 10 week old pup and I was immediately smitten, the pup was good looking, full of life and very friendly. However they refused to let me take the pup until it had been washed and polished etc. So off I went for lunch in the pub while they attended to his toilet.

On my return we loaded him into his box and placed this in the foot well. I said my goodbyes and we headed off on the long journey home. I had barely left the village before the pup was out of the box and clambering all over the passenger seat and doing his best to assist me with the driving, (This was going to be a long journey). For the next 300miles I tried to drive with one hand and tickle the puppy with the other, it's as well the police were not in evidence.

The pup had the ridiculous pedigree name of 'Droolakiss Artful Splodger' and to keep ourselves awake I began to sing "Right said Fred do de do de do do" and this stuck with him and he was now known as 'Freddie'. Well eventually we made it to Cairnhill after a few minor puppy accidents with the cars upholstery. Dottie thought he was wonderful, however Lusso who normally loved everyone and every dog, took an instant dislike to Freddie, probably because he had been the only dog for several months since Bertie died and was now suffering from a touch of jealousy.

Anyway other than Lusso grumbling like mad whenever Freddie came near, everyone settled in very quickly and Freddie and the cat, who was nearly his size became the best of friends. Unfortunately he is now a year old, weighs around 12 stone and thinks he is still the same size as the cat. He constantly chases and corners it and usually manages to cover the cat in droolies which it then spends hours removing. Don't think the cat is persecuted, it could escape anytime it wanted and often spends its time teasing Freddie. If he gets a bit rough it resorts to the good old tactic of the scratched nose. The only time Freddie and Lusso are good friends are when they both have the cat totally cornered and act as a we hate cats posse. However come the evening and the fire is on, unlike in Bertie days they fail to become the best of friends with the cat, still charging around after it and with Freddie sticking his nose out of the cat flap to prevent entry or exit.

We made a mistake with Freddie in that we failed to take him regularly in the car. The only journey made being to the vets for his jabs shortly after his arrival and this probably made him suspicious of cars. When 10 months old I kept trying to get him to go in the car a Nissan X Trail using ramps as the back is quite high, but to no avail. So we decided what he needed was a small van, and so I bought an 11year old van after a month of searching. This is much easier to get into and has a lot of room for both dogs. I have found that if I leave the back doors open Freddie ventures in out of curiosity and if I then shut him in and take the van for a short trip, with a reward walk round the field at the end, he appears to enjoy it. However he then will not go near the van for another 2 days.

We have now owned Freddie for 13 months and I am on the 3rd vacuum cleaner since we got him. We are now on the most expensive high suction cleaner it is possible to buy and the house still manages to look permanently dirty. I should have remembered from our previous St. Bernard's that a clean house is an impossibility once you own one. We have droolies hanging from everywhere including the ceilings and I am always a bit bothered someone will ask to use the bathroom. The toilet is used as a drinking fountain and the associated mess is unbelievable. Freddie is extremely friendly but overpowers every visitor and covers them in slavers, so everyone stays well away.

Just before we got Freddie, I spent around a year building a summer room that faces out over Luse bay. The theory being that in summer we could sit in, out of any breeze and enjoy the view with a glass or two of wine as our only companions. I had just finished the room when Freddie arrived. This had all been painted, side lights fitted and was ready for just the final floor covering and some furniture. I'm glad we hadn't quite finished as on arrival we used the summer room as Freddie's home. He turned out to be the worst dog we have owned in terms of house training and had somehow got it into his head that the summer room was the correct place to 'wee and plop'. Even after 8 months of constantly trying to get him to defecate outside, he would come in from the garden to deliberately 'wee and plop' in the summer room. Needless to say the summer room had a smell all of it's own, even though we were constantly mopping it out. I'm pleased to say that finally we have got through to him and at long last he does everything outside. The other pertinent points with Freddie are that his 'Willie' is constantly out (and it's not tiny), and if asleep his snores would wake the devil.

Other than that he is pretty perfect and intelligent, and we have now owned him for just under a year (He is now 13months old) and I expect to be able to recite many tales about him in years to come.

Freddie

'The big game hunter'

About 30 years ago when I was aged around 35, I was a bit of a 'pretentious git.' At the time I was managing the installation of a range for testing sonorbuoys at Portpatrick.

I used to drive around in an old Silver Cloud Rolls that did between 8 and 12 miles to the gallon. At the time we rented an attractive old farmhouse 'Drumdoch' with a small amount of land. The farmhouse was set in the centre of a dairy farm of several hundred acres.

At the time we had 2 Saint Bernard dogs, 'Jamie' and 'Rex,' plus a collie 'Beth,' a cat, several chickens, geese and a couple of calves 'Fred' and 'Henry'. So we were embracing the country way of life in a big way. I even had a pair of plus fours in which I suspect I looked ridiculous.

At this time I acquired an old Stevens single barrel 12 bore shotgun with which I decided I could supplement a large proportion of our food, and save some money.

It must have been early February as the weather was very cold and a large number of geese had been flying in from Canada. The geese settled each morning in a particular field not far from the house. They usually came in at first light about 6 a.m. I decided a couple would be good for the pot and subsequently got out of bed before 5 a.m. to be prepared.

So as the weather was cold and frosty I wrapped up well and stuffed half a bottle of brandy in my pocket. In the dark I crept down to the field that the geese had landed in for the past week. There was a fairly high hedge around the field and I huddled down out of sight and sat freezing and constantly sipping brandy for the next hour and a half. Suddenly as dawn broke I spotted a great V of incoming geese and slid a cartridge into the breach. The geese came on, exactly on line, and started to descend directly in line with me. Suddenly as I was about to rise and fire they all broke off and circled above me in an 'up yours' sort of formation. Suddenly the swarm broke into two fairly equal parts and smoothly descended into the two fields either side of the one I was in. 'Well out of gun range.' So I decided enough was enough, and they would probably only have been fit for boiling anyway.

A couple of days later I spotted 2 mallards descending onto an overgrown stream. Mallards may not be as big as geese but by god they are tasty. So I donned a pair of waders and taking my trusty un-bloodied gun crept into the stream, 50yards upstream from the ducks. There was plenty of shelter to hide my progress as I slowly crept along the stream, gun cocked, and after getting about half way the depth of water suddenly increased and poured over my waders. However not being one to give up easily I ploughed on, and coming to the final bend I lined up the gun. Breaking through the final reed barrier I suddenly had the ducks bang to rights. But alas there was Daddy duck and there was Mummy duck, and there following neatly behind were six baby ducklings!

So once again I put the gun away never to use it again.

But wait I lie!

Shortly after this episode we decided the farmhouse chimney required cleaning, and being a bright lad I decided to poke the shotgun up the chimney and sort it that way. It certainly worked, clouds of soot fell down onto the sitting room carpet and we spent the next hour cleaning up. However it was only later when we went outside that I realised that the rotating cowl on the top of the chimney pot was now no more than shrapnel devastated scrap.

'As Gladstone said' "No man became great, without many and great mistakes."

🐾

THE TALE OF LUSSO'S TAIL.

(A SHORT TAIL)

Lusso has always been a very friendly and happy dog, and except for the few bad habits that Bertie taut him, intelligent and easily trained. He is a great tail wager and things need to be very wrong before it ever stops.

At this time I had just reached retirement age at 65 but was continuing to work on as I enjoyed my job. I was employed by a German Co. on behalf of the Royal Brunei Navy to maintain the missile radars on 3 corvettes moored at Barrow-in-Furness. I travelled home to Scotland each weekend and resided in a caravan, on a very attractive site near Kirkby-in-Furness during the week. After I had been staying there around 8 months, Lusso came down to stay with me and I found him to be great company, although my caravan was no longer as clean as when I resided on my own. There were several pleasant country pubs in the area that did not object to Lusso coming in, so we would often either have lunch in the pub or pay a short visit on the way home after work. He is very good at breaking the ice, as he will go up to anyone and is very friendly. He is also very good for my health as his main interest and occupation in life is to chase balls, and he will often sit for hours with a ball in his mouth, just waiting for me to throw it. I have seen him chase ducks into the harbour and go in after them with the ball in his mouth. After hopefully swimming round after the ducks he would finally scramble out with the ball still in his mouth. So we would walk over the Cumbria hills and along the beaches by Morecambe bay, and when the sun was shining I would be lazy and sit outside the caravan, throwing balls he would then bring back. He soon found they only got thrown if he brought them back close enough for me not to have to get out of my deck chair. So life was pretty good for both of us, until one day he wagged his tail so hard against a rough wall, he removed the fur from the end and made the tip very sore.

After a couple of weeks it was apparent the tail was not getting better, and in fact appeared to be getting worse. So I took him in to the vet in Stranraer. The vet sighed when he saw it and declared there was nothing worse than dog tails or ears to fix. They decided to clean it up, give him some antibiotic and fit a tube over the end to protect the tail. The tube was made of plastic and held in place with surgical tape. They also fitted him with a large conical collar to prevent him from chewing at his tail.

Both were a bit of a waste of time as we had only been home for about 2 hours before he had totally destroyed the tail tube by wagging it against the wall.

Over the next 4 weeks he went through as many tail protection tubes as I could make and over the following 3 months he totally wrecked about 15 conical collars, all of which were heavily patched by the time they were thrown away.

Around a month after he first had problems with his tail, it was giving him a lot of pain and he incessantly tried to get at it, even though he had his collar on. So I spent my time saying "leave your tailogg alone" (tailogg being how we now referred to his tail.) He was pretty good and tried to leave it alone, even though it was definitely hurting. However I was awakened one morning by some really terrible moans of pain from him and found that the end of his tail seemed to be seeping liquid from within the protective tube. As he was in so much pain I removed the protective tube. He still had his plastic Elizabethan collar on, so I presumed he would be OK. While I was at work on the ships, he would come with me and sit in the back of the car, from which we would go for regular short walks.

He had probably been left to his own devices for around 30 minutes and I decided to let him out for a stroll. Upon arriving at the vehicle, I was assailed by a sight that looked like the aftermath of the Somme offensive. There was blood everywhere within the back of the car and a regular spurt of blood continued to emanate from his tail. He had managed to destroy the plastic collar and had chewed his tail down to the bone. He was now sitting whimpering sadly and obviously expecting me to put things right. I managed to stop the immediate flow of blood and raced him off to a vet in Barrow. As I had never visited the vet previously we had to go through the rigmarole of registering with them before they would attend to him, so by the time he was looked at, the floor was red with blood and one or two of the other folk waiting were beginning to go green at the gills. The vet decided Lusso needed operating on fairly quickly, and the removal of around 6 inches of his tail would be required. I subsequently left him with the Vet, and arranged to pick him up that evening. When I collected him around 5 pm, he was still a bit groggy on his feet and his tail was 6inches shorter. He had a brand new Elizabethan collar and a new tube over his stump. That evening we took life very easily, by relaxing outside my caravan, he being dosed up on heroin and me with a large gin and tonic. The weather at the time in Cumbria was exceptionally good. Lusso had had enough excitement for one day and just decided to sleep. The following day I took off work in order to nurse the poor boy.

He appeared quite happy and wasn't paying much attention to his tail, so I thought we had won. In the morning we threw a few gentle balls for him to retrieve and just after lunch we headed for a quiet country pub that he had been in several times before, "The Prince of Wales" in Foxfield. On every occasion we had visited, normally around 5 pm, there were only a few people in the bar, and it was always friendly. They even had a bowl of water for visiting dogs, and after greeting everyone in the bar Lusso usually lay in front of the log fire.

On this occasion as we entered around 2pm we found the bar packed and very noisy. Anyway Lusso pushed his way through and managed to create chaos with his Elizabethan collar. Amazingly the landlord served me and we retired to the corner with a pint of real ale. Shortly after this, a middle aged woman asked me what I would like to eat, and it was only at this point I realised we had gate crashed a private party. So Lusso and I battled our way out, and headed for home. (The caravan site.)

The evening was spent in the normal way. Sitting admiring the view, whisky in hand, and throwing lots of balls.

The following day I was walking through Barrow town centre, with Lusso on his lead, when this horrendously tough female came up to me in the middle of a crowded street, and started to lambaste me about the sheer cruelty of having a dogs tail docked. She then went on to tell me I was a nasty cruel swine, and then vanished into the crowd of entertained passers by, without giving me time to reply! So feeling guilty for no reason, I crept away. I'd rather be thumped by an 18stone maniacal man than face the likes of her again.

At the weekend after arriving back in Scotland, I took Lusso to our local vet as a matter of courtesy. Upon examining the tail, he declared it sound and dry but indicated that in his opinion the Barrow vet had not left a large enough flap of skin over the wound.

However for a couple of weeks things seemed OK, and other than getting through his plastic collars at the rate of two a week, and a bundle of anti-biotic pills, all seemed well. After around a month it became apparent that all was not well. The tail became infected again, and very soon he was in great pain again. So off to the vet again. The vet decided he would need operating on once more. This could only be the last time, as he would not have enough tail left for a further attempt. I left him with the vet for a week, and this time the job was done by our local Stranraer vet who left a large flap of skin over the wound.

Approximately 3 weeks later his tail looked a lot better and his Elizabethan collar was removed for the first time for 3 months.

The whole episode had an obvious effect on Lusso as he has gone prematurely white around the jaws. It also cost me around £900 and a lot of worry.

Now he is totally back to his normal happy and friendly self, and doesn't appear to miss his tail at all. (He now has just 1.5 inches).

"Luckily we have not met the female ogre again in Barrow".

**NOW A FEW TRUE TALES
OF A LESS PLEASANT TYPE OF ANIMAL.**

'MAN'

"THE WELCOME INN"

Around 5 years ago, I was employed as a contractor, in a well known shipyard, in the west end of Glasgow. At the time the weather was unseasonably hot, and I used to spend a portion of each evening, walking around different areas of the town for exercise. I like Glasgow a lot, and although of English birth, I never came across the reputed anti-English feeling we hear about so much. I always found Glaswegians very friendly, and I love the town. 'I have always believed you should treat people, as you would wish to be treated.'

This particular day was hot and sunny, I had driven into the centre of the town, and started to walk alongside the river Clyde, through what I think used to be called 'Victoria Park'

I was headed in an easterly direction, and after around an hour, was feeling very hot, sweaty, tired and thirsty. I decided I would head away from the park, and stop for a drink in the first pub I came to. The route I took led me back into the east end of Glasgow, an area I was not familiar with!

After around 10 minutes, I arrived at the 'Welcome Inn', a sign outside, indicated that "There were no strangers, in this bar, only friends they were yet to meet". 'Just the job thought I.'

Before entering, it was apparent the bar was fairly full, as I could hear a lot of noise emanating from inside.

In I go, suddenly the entire bar went from very noisy to total silence, there were maybe 15 people in the bar, and all of them were staring at me! The only sound was from the background music, however not wishing to feel intimidated, even though I was as thirsty as hell, I ordered a large scotch, when a glass of orange juice was what I really required. This was served by the barman, without a word, other than to state the amount. From memory I think I was dressed in casual clothes, and my hair as usual was touching my collar. Well I sat there in total silence for about 5 minutes sipping my whisky, and trying to look nonchalant. It was only then that I realised that all the background music was made up of Irish republican songs, some of which mentioned the IRA. At this point I decided the best form of attack was retreat, and downed my drink in one! I left the bar as cheerily as I could, wishing the barman a pleasant good day. Not a word left his lips!

As soon as I vacated the bar, the noise inside became very loud once again, as presumably I was discussed at length.

I can only imagine they thought I was some sort of undercover cop, even though I would have been 61 years old, at the time.

"The Welcome Inn, was undoubtedly the least welcome place I ever remember visiting."

This also reminds me of a pub in Barrow-in -Furness, that I visited one lunchtime, after just arriving there for the first time around 2 years ago.

The pub was like a lot of others in Barrow town centre, it had no real atmosphere, and had the usual 3 or 4 not too desirable looking types, standing by the bar.

I ordered a pint of Guinness , and started to chat about the weather, with a middle aged man, standing next to me at the bar. After about 5 minutes of subsequent relative silence, he burst out with "I know you". "I don't think so says I", anyway he keeps staring at me, until he goes outside for a 'smoke'.

Meanwhile I finish my second pint of beer, and decide to head off back to work. Who do I encounter, as I leave, but the man who thinks he knows me!

As I am leaving he jumps out and says "I know who you are" "You're CID".

Considering I had only days before arrived in Barrow, had hair down to my neck, and was by then aged 64, I should have taken this as a compliment.

"You are cleverer than you look" say I, "But don't forget we've got our eye on you"

'I never went back to that pub'

"This makes it sound as though Barrow is an unpleasant place. In actual fact it is one of the friendliest places I have ever been, and although the town centre pubs are a bit basic, by the time you travel 2 miles outside the town, it is exceptionally pleasant.

"A visit to HMS Sheffield"

' In the following tale the names of all concerned have been changed to save the guilty.'

I was sitting at my desk in Frimley, Surrey, where I was employed as Chief trials engineer for the Marconi Co. when word came through that HMS Sheffield needed urgent assistance with their Seawolf missile radar. The ship at the time was on 'Armilla' patrol in the Arabian Gulf. The first Gulf war had finished just months before. At the time I resided in a cottage within the Pembrokeshire national park in Wales, and had promised to take my wife to the County show in Haverfordwest the following Saturday. So as today was Tuesday and I needed to be back in Wales for Friday, I booked a BA flight to Dubai for overnight Wednesday with a flight back early on Friday morning giving me one full day to investigate the ships problems. I then arranged for the Military Attaché from the Dubai embassy to meet me at the airport on arrival, and arrange to get me to the ship. I also booked myself into the Jebal Ali hotel for Thursday night.

Everything went according to plan initially. I was given a seat in the bubble on top of the 747 and managed to obtain a few hours sleep on the overnight journey. We landed in Dubai around 8 am, and having cleared customs, I went in search of the British military attaché. As we came down the elevator there were lots of people carrying placards with names on them, however I could not find anyone meeting me! After around 30 minutes and finding everyone else had gone, and not having the embassy telephone number, I decided the only thing I could do was to try and find HMS Sheffield moored somewhere in the Jebal Ali docks. So I go and try to find a taxi and was approached by an Arab in traditional dress, who grabbed my bag and charged off to a car in the general car park. As soon as we arrived he shot out of the car park, without asking where I was going, and suspicion of being kidnapped shot through my mind. However as soon as we cleared the airport, he reached under his seat and produced a taxi sign, which he stuck on his roof. So I had managed to collect a rogue taxi. Then the language barrier set in, he didn't understand my request to find HMS Sheffield, so we fell back on the second option of going to the Jebal Ali hotel. Only now did I realise how large the Jebal Ali docks were, they went on for mile after mile, and it also became plain that the driver didn't know where the hotel was. He stopped at every hotel we came across, and asked if this was it? Thank god eventually we arrived at the correct one. I then asked how much the fare was, and he gave me a figure approx equal to £7. The smallest note I possessed was equal to around £25 sterling. (A not inconsiderable sum in 1991). He, of course, had no change, and said he would get the note changed while I booked in. Of course, by the time I had booked in, both he and my note were long gone. "This was just the start".

The hotel had an old fashioned type exchange, with a girl sitting in it. She managed to put me through to the British embassy, and I was then put through to the Military attaché, who was full of apologies and stated that they had totally forgotten I was coming. He arranged for a taxi to take me to the ship, and while I was waiting, I booked an early call and a taxi for 4 am the following morning. My flight was for 6 am.

The taxi arrived and transported me to the ship with no problem. Upon arrival I was met by a Lt. Commander, the Weapons Engineering Officer (WEO), and the Radar tracker maintainer, a Chief Petty Officer (CPO).(Who we will call Bob). The WEO was an ex submariner and famous throughout the fleet as a bit of a sod. The first question he asked me was how long do you plan to stay. When I said "I'm Flying back in the morning" he became very agitated and said I certainly wasn't, as his 'Maintainer' had been trying to resolve the problem for 3 months and how do you think you can fix it in a day. My reply was that if I hadn't fixed it by the end of the day, it wasn't going to be fixed.

Anyhow to cut a short story even shorter, I had found the problem and resolved it in about 1 hour. I demonstrated the repair to the Deputy WEO, and now it was Bobs turn to get agitated. He told me that he was going to be in 'deep shit' with the WEO for not locating the problem. 'I told him I would try and think of something.'

Shortly afterwards, the Deputy WEO, Bob (the maintainer) and myself were invited to a meeting with the WEO in the Wardroom.

Upon arrival the WEO asked me if I would like a coffee! He then poured 3 coffee's, one for the Deputy WEO, one for himself, and one for me. He pointedly did not pour one for Bob, so I knew at this point he really was in trouble. "How come you have resolved the problem so quickly, and my maintainer couldn't." was his first question. I could have replied truthfully, "Because he's incompetent" but what's the point?

Instead I started to lie through my teeth. "I don't believe your maintainer, would ever find this type of problem, without the use of specialist test equipment, I brought out with me." says I.

"And what form does this equipment take". said the WEO.

" Special development test boards for the 'Tracker processor unit" says I.

Now I thought I'm also in the deep end, as he is going to ask to see them, ('and they were residing in my desk in Frimley, Surrey.') But luckily he was happy with my answer and thanked me for coming at such short notice.

Once we left the Wardroom, Bob told me how grateful he was, and would I join him for a drink in the Chiefs Mess. On entering the mess, which was quite full, Bob immediately told all his mates how I had saved his neck, and that they should ensure I was well entertained. It must have been about 1 pm by now, and pints of cider started to build up around me. I was extremely tired and almost ready for my bed, but it would have been extremely churlish to refuse their hospitality, as they were also good company. The second problem I had is that I had not eaten since the aircraft, and was soon feeling the effects of the cider. By around 4 pm, I requested a taxi to get me back to the hotel, only to be told there was no point, as they were going out for the night, and a minibus was due shortly to pick everyone up. They stated that they would drop me off at the hotel in passing! 'What a fool I was.'

Well we all clambered into the minibus, and off we go! But as you might guess it went nowhere near my hotel. Instead we headed for some bar, where they had arranged a darts match with some local ex-pats. I honestly don't remember much about that evening, but believe I enjoyed myself, and was eventually dropped off at my hotel around midnight.

Still sitting on my bed was the case I had dropped off unopened on arrival. I dived into bed, and slept until my early call at 4 am. Packing was easy as all I had to do was collect my unopened suitcase. The flight back was uneventful, but I still had to drive from Heathrow airport to my home in Wales. A journey of about 180 miles. I got as far as the Severn Bridge, and with a hundred miles still to go, booked into the Severn Lodge and slept for the next15 hours or so. I arrived back home just in time to take Dottie to the County show.

Since then I have always been very wary when invited out by that fine bunch of lads from the Royal Navy!

🐾

'A VISIT TO HMS CAMPBELTOWN'

Once again I was involved with the Royal Navy. This time it was to carry out 'Blast' trials on HMS Campbeltown, to asses the effect of firing the 4.5 inch gun on the radar dishes. At the time Campbeltown, a batch 3 Type 22 frigate had been newly commissioned, and so was considered one of the R.N.'s finest vessels. HRH The Duke of York. (Prince Andrew) being the resident helicopter pilot.

We (The civilian contingent) had spent around 3 months preparing for the trials, by fitting 'Blast sensors and vibration sensing equipment' to all the radar dishes. The trials were conducted off the western approaches to Plymouth, around mid summer. (Extremely unusual, as the navy always plans their trials for the summer, but ends up conducting them in the January/ February gales, after inevitable delays, they always blame on the civilian contractors.).

We were day running from Plymouth, for about 4 days to conduct the trials. As civilians we spent the night in hotels, and were then picked up by a 'Pas' boat early in the morning and taken out to the ship. We were to be picked up from Milbay docks near the centre of Plymouth. While we were hanging around waiting for the boat to pick us up, I went for a short stroll along the quayside, where there were several small fishing boats, offloading their fish. After I had wandered up and down a few times, observing the fishermen throwing some of their catch back into the sea, I went back to join my chums.

Shortly afterwards a fisherman approached me and asked who I was. "Just waiting for a boat," I said. "Bloody Hell" says he, "We have just thrown half our catch back, we thought you were the damned fisheries inspector."

On board HMS Campbeltown, the weather was good to us, except visibility was very poor due to fog. This did not deter the brave lads of Her Majesties Navy, we fired round after round of 4.5 inch shells into the fog, relying on the navigation radar to be sure the coast was clear. I often wonder how many Spanish fishing vessels went to the bottom that day.

As civilians on a R.N. ship, we normally enjoy a drink or two at lunchtime, in the Wardroom. However on this ship, the 'First Lieutenant' (Why they call him that god alone knows, as he his usually a Lt. Commander or above.) refused to open the bar, stating that it was not done on his ship. That didn't improve our mood, being stuck at sea is bad enough. Still we visited the 'Chiefs Mess' instead where the men are less up their own backsides.

Now lunch was over and we had finished firing for the day, the ships crew instead of going back, decided to have a 'Man overboard' exercise. This involved throwing a blow up doll overboard, (the navy always seemed to have a never ending supply of these!) and then pressing a button that fired a lifebelt and a flare close to the body. To save money they did not fire the flare but just threw a lifebelt over the side. The ship then sailed off, swung round in a large circle, and returned to pick up the body, (Blow up doll). However on returning they could not find it, and sailed up and down looking, with no luck. (one of the civilians on board spotted the doll on the horizon, but we failed to let the crew know, as they had failed to open the bar.)

The next day, after we had finished the trials for the day, the crew decided they had better repeat the 'Man overboard exercise' and this time do it properly. They threw over the rubber doll, and this time fired the Flare and lifebelt. Once again, off goes the ship, swings round and pulls alongside the body. 'Perfect'.

The rescue crew then climb into the rubber ships boat, and then start to lower the boat down to the sea. Halfway down, there was suddenly a mighty splash, as the boats outboard motor fell off, and vanished to the bottom of the blue. Eventually, after maybe 30 minutes. They sent the swimmer of the day, to collect the blow-up doll, lifebelt and flare.

('The only thing I have ever learnt from the Navy is "Don't fall overboard."')

After 4 days we had completed the trials programme, I had a small problem with one of the radars, but could not attend to it, as the ship was sailing round to Portland that evening.

So I arranged to drive round to Portland, and look into the problem, the following day.

I arrived on the ship post lunch, and set to work to resolve the problem. Generally the ship was deserted, other than watch keepers, as everyone else appeared to be on shore leave. The radar problem was proving more difficult to resolve than I had expected, and I was still there in the early evening. Feeling ready for a coffee, I headed down to the wardroom. On Type 22 frigates there is a long staircase down from the upper deck to the wardroom. As I was descending a naval officer in uniform was coming up the opposite way. (Now remember I had just spent 4 days at sea with the crew), and I vaguely recognised him. As I passed him I said "Hi Mate", and he replied in a rather surprised tone with "Hi". As I sat down in the wardroom, with my cup of coffee, it suddenly struck me who he was!

*******On reflection I now suspect that "Hi Mate" is probably not the correct way to address a senior member of 'The Royal Family' on the first meeting.********

DENZIL BY NAME.

In the mid 1970's while installing a Sonobuoy range in Portpatrick in Scotland, I spent a lot of time working with MOD personnel, who were manning and running the test range. Part of the range equipment was a converted ex RAF air/sea rescue launch, the 'Aquilla Maris.' The crew were a good bunch of lads, consisting of the skipper Pete and 4 deck hands. One of the deck hands was a lad of around 19years old, called Denzil. He was probably not the brightest lamp around, and was known to the crew as 'Denzil by name, Denzil by nature.'

An example of his power of thought, can be seen by this small episode. He and his mate, decided to 'Do the village shop,' in Portpatrick. They must have been watching a few movies, as they carried out a very professional job. They carefully cut a round piece of glass out of the door, so they could reach in and open the latch. They then carried out their robbery of the shop, and got away undetected.

However the following morning, the 'Old Bill' turned up, and charged them. The investigation had not taken too long, as all the police had to do, was ask the proprietor, what was missing! Subsequently they only needed to ask around, as to who smoked Rothmans King size. 'As this was all they had taken.'

Anyway, the main aspect of this following story, kept everyone on the range amused for some time. But with hindsight, it was a bit cruel.

The lads on the range decided to call Denzil up for 'National service', (Now remember no one had been called up since 1960, and this was the mid seventies.). In this period, computer systems were still very expensive, and rare. We had a 'main frame' Hewlet Packard system on the range, and this is what the lads used to generate the call-up papers. I can't remember the exact details, but the call-up papers went something like this. Firstly they had fancy government type headings and crests, and a simple text;

"You are to report to the Edinburgh barracks of the Black Watch, on Monday the 1st of May 1976, in order to complete your National Service, for a period of 18 months.

We will arrange to meet you at Waverley Station at 10am. Please bring only essential items.

Failure to comply, will result in prosecution for dereliction of duty.

Signed; Colonel J.McKie Officer commanding.

This call-up notice was posted to the boat as Registered mail. Along with Denzils call-up papers, Pete the skipper of the boat, also received documents, allowing him to release Denzil from service as a crew member. (Pete, of course, was aware of the scam.).

Denzil, received his documents on the boat, and did not appear too surprised, just a bit worried about what the future held for him. Pete, also showed him the letter authorising his release. When he went home in the evening, as they were sat around the dinner table, he showed his call-up papers to his Dad. Instead of saying, "You silly sod, there is no National service." He said "Good, it will make a man of you". I still don't know if his Dad was aware it was a scam, or if it was a case of 'like farther, like son'. I suspect the latter.

The date of his call-up was something like 6 weeks away, and as time moved on he became more and more agitated. On one occasion, he showed his documents, to one of the range lads, John, who said "You poor sod, I served under Colonel McKie, when I was in, and he was a complete swine."

Eventually things started to get out of hand, and Denzil was fully preparing to leave. The final straw, was when he placed his motorcycle in the local paper under 'For Sale'. At this point the joke had gone too far, and the lads had to generate more documents, to defer his National service. Supposedly thanks to the intervention of Pete the skipper, who had written indicating that he was doing a job, of great value to the nation, and couldn't be spared.

Along with his deferment papers, Pete the skipper was sent a covering letter, indicating his release from National service, but stating that as Denzil was still subject to military law, the skipper of the boat, the 'Aquilla Maris', would be entitled to punish any misdeeds, by administering up to 5 lashes!

I believe Denzil became a model crew member from here on in.

On a separate occasion, his fellow crew members, carried out another practical joke on him.

Approximately every 6 months, a nurse hired by the range, visited the 'Aquilla Maris' to check on the health and well being of the crew. One of the crew members, who went in before Denzil, said to the nurse as she was leaving, " I think Denzil may have something to tell you, he thinks he's got V.D., but doesn't like talking about it".

Well, when Denzil went in to see the nurse, she asked him all the usual questions, and then at the end, asked him if he had anything else he was worried about? Of course he said no, so she persevered, confusing him more and more. Eventually she realised, she had been had, but I don't think Denzil, ever knew what it was all about.

'I haven't seen Denzil for a long time, but hope the world is treating him well!'

🐾

A VISIT TO THE BRITISH EMBASSY IN BERN.

Around 1973, I was involved with the first demonstrations, of the Rapier missile system to the Swiss. The British Aircraft Corporation, were the prime contractors, and had a team of around 15 people out in country. I was employed at the time as a fairly junior member, of the 5 man Marconi Space and Defence Systems group, sub-contracting to BAC.

The demonstration trials, were being conducted at a Swiss Procurement authority compound, not far from Lucerne. Shortly after arrival, it was necessary to erect a tower, around 300metres, from the compound boundary, in order to house target and missile simulators. The Swiss undertook to carry out this task, and hired contractors, to build the tower from a form of scaffolding. By the end of the week, the tower was almost complete, was around 30 meters high, and had a nice hut placed on top, to house our equipment.

The Swiss did not like working weekends, so come Friday afternoon, we all went off until Monday morning.

Upon arriving back on the site, where once had stood a magnificent tower, we observed nothing but a pile of twisted and tangled scaffolding.

'This just shows that no matter how important, the Swiss ministry guys thought they were, they were no match for an angry farmer, with a powerful tractor, who's permission, they had failed to obtain, before erecting the tower on his land.'

Once these minor problems were resolved, the trials started in earnest. The Swiss threw all their fastest, and latest aircraft at us. These included French Mirages, British Hunters, etc; we successfully acquired and tracked, all these targets, with the missile system, without problems. However we had one flaw, in our system at the time. Any target going less than around 90 miles per hour, was not considered a threat. The Swiss spotted this minor defect, and attacked the site with an ancient spotter plane, that only did about 60 miles per hour. The aircraft could be seen, and heard, by everyone, from many miles away, however all we could do was sit and watch it leisurely approach, as the radar system, continually rejected it as a 'non threat.' Eventually the old bi-plane, was directly above the site, and calmly dropped a 5 pound bag of flour, onto us all. (we learnt several lessons from this!).

On another occasion, the slow target programming obviously failed, as we locked onto, and tracked, an eagle. The Swiss were quite pleased with this, as they had radar controlled film of the eagle, with its mate circling round it. In spite of some of these minor problems, the customer was very pleased with the system, and bought them for many years to come.

Around 2 months into the demonstration period, I was asked to go to the British Embassy in Bern, in order to deliver, trials results, for return to the UK, in the diplomatic bag.

I arranged to meet the Military Attaché, and set off in a hire car to Bern.

Upon arrival, I was met by the Attaché, who escorted me, up the stairs, and along a corridor, several inches deep in carpet, and with walls covered by oil paintings, of Waterloo, Trafalgar etc. We arrived at his office, where it was apparent, his previous visitor had just left, as the remains of the tea were still on his desk. The tea service was silver and the cups were of fine bone china.

After a short discussion, on how the demonstration was going, I handed over the documents, and he asked me if I would like some tea. "Yes" I replied, thinking someone would bring in another tray of fine silver and china. 'Not a chance'. We left his office, and continued on down the gold plated corridor. Suddenly at the end, the corridor turned right. The contrast was unbelievable! The fancy carpet and paintings, turned into whitewash and lino. A short distance along this path we arrived at a room, where the noise level, even with the door shut, was tremendous. Upon opening the door, we were greeted by the entire embassy staff, enjoying their tea break. I was introduced to a very friendly and attractive Swiss girl, who it turned out was secretary to the Ambassador. She invited me to partake of tea and biscuits, and went off to make me a cup. Upon returning, I was presented with my tea, in a very large cracked mug, the sort with blue bands around it. I commented on the fact that I was surprised, this was the best, the British Embassy, appeared to be able to supply!

'Only to be told that I was extremely honoured, to be drinking from it, as it was the 'Ambassadors personal mug', and he was away for the day.'

During our 3 month stay in Switzerland, we were given the use of a minibus, in order to sightsee. On one weekend 5 of us decided to do Europe in a day. (A sort of Yanks tour). Our plan was to start in Italy, however the tunnel was shut, with heavy snow, so we started in Austria, (the requirement for having seen a country was to have a pint of beer, and send a postcard), then did Liechtenstein, Germany, Belgium, and France. So including Switzerland, we 'toured' 6 nations in a day. We ended up in the evening, in a restaurant near Basel, where we ordered, Cheese Fondue, washed down with vast quantities of Algerian red plonk. The owner advised us not to drink red wine with Fondue, but being Brits we knew better. Subsequently we spent the next 2 days in agony.

The other, useful thing about Basel, was the fact that it crossed the Swiss/French border, and we found that if we filled the van up on the French side, we could then present the receipt, to BAC Ltd. who would then pay us back in Swiss franks. The Swiss frank at the time, being worth around 4 French franks. The scam only came unstuck, when they eventually realised, the van tank did not take 50 gallons. 'From there onwards BAC refused to pay any further petrol bills.   'So they had the last laugh'.

LORD WINESTOCK VISITS EASTWOOD HOUSE.

Alenia Marconi Ltd. had just opened a new headquarters building, 'Eastwood House', in Chelmsford.

I at the time was working at Frimley, in Surrey, but visited Chelmsford, on a weekly basis. It was mid summer at the time, and as I had no meetings to attend, I was dressed in an open necked shirt, and slacks. As I pulled into the visitors car park, in my old Jaguar, a very posh limousine, pulled in next to me. As I was not an employee of Chelmsford, I always used the main visitors entrance, which was carefully guarded by a very attractive young lady 'Jo', with whom I had become friends, over a short period of time.

As I got out of my car, a chauffeur opened the Door, for a short, smartly dressed man, I vaguely recognised. Along with him, was a very large woman, who gave me a stare, that would have put a candle out at 50 metres. Anyway not taking too much notice, I continued on towards the front entrance, with the limousines passengers following a few paces behind.

When I reached the front entrance, I should have realised something was not normal, standing smartly to attention, at the entrance was a doorman. (Something they did not normally have!). With a rather surprised look on his face, he held the door open for me. 'Strait through goes I', only to find myself, facing 6 Company directors, all with their hands held out, ready to shake mine. This threw the whole episode into chaos, the directors broke up in confusion, just as their real visitor appeared through the door. Meanwhile I was placed under arrest by Jo, and stuffed in a corner. Looking up, I spotted a large screen that stated;

"Eastwood House, Welcomes, Lord Winestock to our grand opening."

Meanwhile the Co. Directors, had more or less, sorted themselves out, and after greeting 'Arnie' (Lord Winestock), were now escorting him through the second set of doors, into the vestibule. The directors now congregated, by the lift, and while they were waiting for it to come down, Lord Winestock, scampered up the stairs. This now threw them into more chaos, and they scampered after him. (I like to think he did it on purpose, to bring them down to earth!)

Once they had gone, I was released by Jo, and continued up to the second floor, where I was met by Beverly the secretary, who curtsied to me. (Not more than 5 minutes had gone by, but everyone already knew of the incident!).

'I subsequently heard that 'Lord Winestock' had commented that it was one of the more fun days of his life, but don't know if that was true'.

🐾

The 'Big Robbery'

I only heard this story second hand, so can't guarantee its authentic content. In the early 1970's, in Stranraer, there were a number of small filling stations. The town was a very safe place to live, there being almost no real crime. These days there are a few 'Druggies', however it is still a pleasant area to live in.

Anyway back in the 1970's, robbery with violence, was unheard of, although the IRA used the ferry link to Belfast, as a means of smuggling in arms. In one instance, a bag of high explosive was found in the cistern, of the public toilets, at the railway station.

A regular acquaintance of mine, (I won't use the term friend) who I shall call Dougie, had a small motor vessel, and used to do a little smuggling to Northern Ireland. Not arms, but in those days there were shortages over there of fairly normal commodities, and the overnight transfer of these items could be quite profitable.

On one occasion, at night, Dougie was just leaving the Clyde estuary, bound for Belfast, when a fast launch, appeared behind him. The launch drew close, and switched on it's spotlight. "Heave to, Dragonfly, H.M. Customs" was called over the 'loud hailer,' and Dougie, realising he was in a bit of a predicament, started to throw stuff overboard. Suddenly, laughter started to emanate from the 'loud hailer', and one of his so called friends, from the other launch, said "Got you that time, Dougie".

Anyway, one late evening in Stranraer, the girl, who was on duty at the filling station, was just locking up. Suddenly a figure clad in a terrorist style balaclava, the sort where only the eyes and mouth show, appeared and in a very threatening voice said, "Hand over the cash". Being a very brave sort, the girl replied "No". This left the thief in a quandary, as he waved his replica gun around, and he started to bluster, and threaten. Still getting nowhere, and the girl bravely holding her ground, he did a runner.

Subsequently the police arrived, and questioned the girl! Had she any idea who it might have been?

"Oh yes" she replied, "He was my next door neighbour, I recognised his voice!"

🐾

Guides and Markers.

Back in 1970, I was a Senior NCO, in the Royal Air Force. The technical branches, of the RAF, have never been very good at things like marching, and I was particularly bad at drill, having 2 left feet. At the time I was stationed at RAF Patrington, a Ground Radar Station. The domestic camp, was situated around 20 miles from the city of Hull, in Yorkshire. By tradition the RAF paraded through the city, every 'Remembrance' day, and on this occasion, I had been lucky enough to have been selected, to appear on the parade.

Rehearsals for the parade, were conducted, every Sunday morning, for around a month prior to the official parade. The main body of the parade was made up of 3 ranks, of junior airmen. One SNCO then took the position of 'Guide' at the front of the column, and one SNCO, then became the 'Marker', at the rear of the column. I was designated as the 'Marker'.

None of us had done any real drill, for several years, but after 4 weekends of practice, we were passable. The practice sessions, were commanded by a 'Warrant Officer', and consisted of 'forming up', several streets away from our final destination, at the 'War Memorial'. After forming up we were commanded, to 'Left turn', and then marched through the streets of Hull, with the 'Guide' leading the way, and me as the

'Marker' taking up the rear. Upon arrival at the War memorial, the 'Guide' then took up his allocated position, and the rest of the column, then formed up/halted neatly behind him. It looked as though we would carry off the day, without an excess of embarrassment.

The day of the parade arrived, the only difference being, that a 'Commissioned' officer, now commanded the parade, in place of the previous 'Warrant officer'. Now as every NCO knows, in order to become commissioned, every potential officer, must have half his brain removed.

Initially, all went well, we formed up, as previously, on the same street. The 'commissioned officer' then inspected the parade, and declared himself satisfied.

That's where the sensible bit ended. The officer in charge, gave out the command, "Right turn". The parade obeyed. This now meant, we were not only facing the wrong way, but I had suddenly been promoted to 'Guide'. Instead of admitting the mistake, and about turning the column, we continued in the wrong direction. I had lived in Hull, for around a year, and so had a rough idea of where we were. I led the column, down a couple of streets, that I thought would bring us out at the memorial. However it soon became clear, that the route was not filled with cheering spectators, just a few mums, pushing prams. Eventually I managed to head the column in approximately the right direction, and we were back on route. Upon arrival at the 'War memorial', I led the parade neatly passed the memorial, and stopped at what appeared to be the correct spot. The parade halted, behind me. Unfortunately the back end of the column, was still sitting in the middle of the road. So we all shuffled-up raggedly, until we were in position. Luckily it had not quite struck 11am, when the ceremony was due to commence.

Everything now went O.K. and after the service, we formed up again, and marched in good order, to the 'British Legion' club, where free beer was on offer. (I must have met with approval, as a 'Guide' as the column was once again formed the wrong way round.) Some of the old soldiers, took the 'Mickey' out of our, performance, while others said they hadn't had as big a laugh, at a 'Remembrance' parade before.

'Still with several pints of their 'good ale' inside us we didn't really care!'

A Weekend in Beirut.

I was stationed, on top of the Troodos mountains, in Cypress, back in the mid 1960's.

At the time, it was possible to fly from Nicosia, to Beirut, for around £12 each way. However, at the time, Beirut was strictly speaking, out of bounds, to British forces. This was before all the civil war, between the Christians and Muslims. Beirut, being an ex-French colony, was considered to be the Monte-Carlo, of the Middle east. The weather was generally very good. There were a number of international standard, hotels, and lots of good restaurants. It was possible to water ski in the morning, and then drive up into the mountains, to ski on snow in the afternoon. The town was divided into 2 halves. The European end, and the Arab quarter, where there were a number of 'souks' and cheap hotels. Alcohol was readily available and very cheap.

The fact that Beirut was out of bounds, made trips there, all the more exciting. So we would fly over on a Friday, stay in some ghastly, cheap Arab hotel, and fly back Sunday.

Prior to this particular visit, I had just purchased, a very expensive, twin lens reflex camera, from the Naafi, on a year's hire purchase.

On this particular visit, I was accompanied by the self styled. 'Tiger Harris of the Middle East'. Tiger was in fact, about 5ft 6inches tall, and weighed in at around 9 stone. However he could talk the hind leg, off a donkey.

The weekend started normally, a drink in several bars, and ending up in the St. George hotel, bar. This was quite posh, and didn't really prepare us, for our return to the Arab quarter, doss house, in which we were staying. Our hotel was situated in 'The plas de- Matre' and had noisy, constant passing traffic, throughout the night. The next day we did a bit of sightseeing, including, walking through the Arab markets, with one hand firmly over our passports. In those days, there were no credit cards, or cheque guarantee cards. So we needed to ensure, we always had adequate funds, with us. Being British forces overseas, our idea of adequate funding, would be about £2, more than we expected to spend.

On our 2nd day in country, Saturday, we had had a most enjoyable time, and had just started to head back to our hotel, when a young Arab, carrying a tray of items, on a string hanging round his neck, appeared. He went close up to Tiger, and poking his tray, into Tigers chest, asked if we wanted to buy anything. The answer was "No". He appeared resigned, and slowly walked away. Once he had put some distance, between us, he suddenly burst into a sprint, and vanished up an alley. At this point we knew something was wrong. 'Tiger found his wallet missing!' This was a disaster, as we now, did not have enough money between us, to pay the hotel, and get back to Cypress. (Remember we were also in a country that was out of bounds, to the RAF). The only asset we had between us, was my nice new, shiny camera. We spent the rest of the day, attempting to sell the camera, by going from shop to shop. However none of the Wiley, French trained Arabs, would offer us enough to get home. Eventually we had to go back to the hotel, and tell the Arab owner, we couldn't pay the bill. With less than good grace, he accepted the camera in lieu, of the bill. We now had nowhere to sleep, for the last night, and ended up at Beirut airport, sleeping on the benches.

Eventually we flew out of Beirut, for Nicosia, around 2 in the afternoon. When we arrived in Nicosia, there was great excitement, within the airport. Approximately 1 hour after we flew out, Israeli special forces, had flown into Beirut airport, and blown up all the aircraft, on the ground.   'Were we lucky'.

'To add injury to the experience, I was still paying for a camera I didn't own for the next 12 months.' I never visited Beirut again!

Burglar Alarms

In about 1975, I had a small part time business, making and fitting, burglar alarms. In those days, both infra red and radar alarms, were fairly new and expensive. I designed and built my own version of a radar detector, but bought in the infra red devices.

The very first system, I installed, was in a Chinese restaurant. I had spent many hours, at home testing the system to ensure, there were not too many 'false alarms'. Being my first commission, I was extremely naive, and spent a couple of evenings, installing the equipment. As the restaurant was always busy, until late at night, I could not really carry out any installation tests. However like a fool, I thought, I've tested everything, at home, so we shouldn't have any problems. The other silly thing I did, was to connect the siren, before testing. I also fitted a digital, 'false alarm' counter, and left this in their window, so I could check on any problems, the next morning. I left the owner with instructions, on how to set the alarm, as he closed up shop.

The next morning, I confidently, approached the restaurant window, to check there were no false alarms. My enthusiasm was seriously punctured, when I observed on the 'false alarm' counter, not the zero, I was expecting, but 127. It turned out the local constabulary, and most of the local residents, had been up half the night, with the constant, din of the siren.

I now spent, several evenings, attempting to resolve the problem, and carried out a few modifications, only to find, the alarm was still going off overnight. 'The siren had now been disconnected, so the locals could sleep well'. I decided, the only way I would resolve the problem, was by remaining in the restaurant, overnight. So around 1am, the staff vacated the premises, leaving me alone. By 2am, I had resolved the problem, I had made the radar detectors, far too sensitive, they were picking up the movement of 'Rodents coming out to dine!'

I installed several systems, after this, without problems, but then I obtained my biggest job to date. The owner of a local cash and carry, gave me the task of protecting his warehouse, where there had been several cases, of thieves, breaking in through the roof, and stealing alcohol. Along with the warehouse, he asked me to fit an alarm system to the adjacent garage, used for servicing the delivery lorries.

I spent a long time, designing and building, the system, which used a combination of radar, infra red and reed switches. The system was also fitted with a 999 dialling machine.

With the assistance of a friend, the installation to both the warehouse and garage, was completed in around 1 week. Having by now learnt a few lessons, the 999 dialler was initially not connected. After running the system, for several days, with no false alarms, I connected the 999 dialler.

All went well, for a few days, then my phone rang, indicating a break-in, at the warehouse. By the time I arrived, there were 3 police cars, approx 10 policemen, and a copper on a bike, plus the owner, standing around outside. I entered the building, and located the zone, the alarm had gone off in. No sign of any break-in. The system was reset, and worked without problems for a week, after which the alarm, once again went off. This time when I arrived, there was only 1 police car, plus the copper on the bike, and the owner. On investigation, the same sensor had been tripped. I changed this infra red sensor, for a spare, in case it was faulty. All went well again for a further week, until, one again the alarm went off. This time when I arrived, there was just the copper on the bike, plus the owner, and once again the same sensor had been triggered. I then realised, the only time the alarm went off, was a Thursday evening. Upon investigation, it turned out that Thursday was the big delivery day, and the only time the warehouse was empty. Normally the delivery lorries were left outside, but as the warehouse was empty on a Thursday, they parked them in the building. 'The rapid cooling of the lorry engines, was enough to trigger the alarm'. After this we had no more trouble, the lorries were left outside.

Shortly after this, I was called out, by the fitter who worked in the adjacent garage. The garage alarm was operating continually. Upon arrival, I was confronted by chaos, the siren was sounding away, and the interconnecting alarm wiring, was in tatters. It turned out that the mechanic, had returned off 2 weeks holiday, and couldn't remember the security code, for the alarm system. So after a few futile attempts, to stop the alarm, he cut every wire he could see. Of course this did no good, as the siren was a self contained unit, once triggered. It took me longer to repair the damage, than the original installation.

"We all learn by other peoples mistakes."

One of my installations, was around 20 miles away, in a little cottage, in Ayrshire. The owner was a really nice old man, with a wife suffering from multiple sclerosis. The alarm worked well, for over a year, after which I was called out. Upon arrival, I found a fairly disastrous situation. There had been a storm the night before, and a lightning strike, had struck the alarm system. I removed the full system, and spent several days rebuilding it.   This was then re-installed, and retested. The old gentleman, kindly gave me a bottle of German white wine, for my efforts. 'Not bad for a weeks work'. However I was glad I had received it gratefully, not long afterwards, as he rang me to say the alarm was sounding again. I drove out to investigate, and found the couple were just about to go on holiday. At this point, I should have disabled the siren, however I told him it would soon flatten the internal battery, and we would investigate the problem, on his return.

Around 3 days later, I was called to his house, by the police, only to find there had been a break-in, by what appeared to have been a tramp. Very little of value, had been stolen, but a bit of a mess was left. However the siren after 3 days was still quietly, singing to itself, making it obvious to the tramp no one was in. Also present was the owners son in law, who happened to be a solicitor! The owner when he returned, persuaded his son in law, that further action was not needed, and I then resolved the alarm problem. By now I was totally fed-up with being called out at night, and dealing with the general public. Although I have to say, most of them were very nice people. I gave up the alarm business, and went into disco. 'But that's another story'.

🐾

A VISIT TO HMS LONDON

Just prior to the first Gulf war, HMS London, the British flotilla flagship, had just completed a number of Seawolf missile firings, on its way round to the Arabian Gulf. These had been singularly unsuccessful, with all the missiles, acting more like torpedoes.

As the ship was the 'Flagship', this was likely to affect the entire operation, if the ship had to return to the U.K. In view of this, the Admiralty Surface Weapons Establishment, (ASWE), at Portsmouth, decided to send a team out urgently, to resolve the problem. We had just returned from the Christmas/New year holidays, and the war was due to start mid-January. A team of 'volunteers', was rapidly assembled. This consisted of a R.N. Commander, from ASWE, an ex R.N. Lt Commander, from Captain Weapons Trials, (CWT), Trevor, a friend of mine from Marconi, Chelmsford, who were the prime contractors, for the missile radars, and myself representing the main sub-contractor. Both the Naval officers were called Mike, and they both hated each other, which made for a good start. (I shall call them Mike G. and Mike M.).

All 4 of us converged separately, then met up, on a military supply base, near Cheltenham. Here we were issued with gas and biological, protection gear. They attempted to also issue us with guns and sleeping bags, which we declined. Afterwards, I wished we had taken them up on the sleeping bags.

We then drove in convoy, to RAF Lyneham, where we parked our cars, and prepared to fly out.

The flight out was uneventful, but interesting, in that we were almost the only passengers, other than a couple of Land Rovers, and things that looked awfully like bombs. We were well attended to, by a couple of RAF air stewardesses, who weren't exactly picked for their looks, but plied us with innumerable, soft drinks and food. We landed in Riyadh, Saudi Arabia, around 1 am local time. The brand new Riyadh airport, had been totally taken over by the military, and was a mass of F15's, Tornadoes and Hercules, constantly taking off and landing. This is where our plans started to go wrong! We had intended staying in 5 star hotels, throughout our visit, but found no one was allowed off the base. This is where a sleeping bag would have been nice, as the only accommodation was the floor. Alcoholic drink was definitely not available, and catering was like you would expect on a battle field. We were due to fly to Dubai, by Hercules, at 09-00hrs, so tried to find a clear spot on the floor, along with a vast number of army types. I had just settled down nicely and finally gone to sleep, under a pile of cardboard boxes, when the most almighty din broke out. An entire regiment, of highland troops, in kilts, led by a pipe band, marched regally through, the entire airport, departure lounge, as if they were heading for Culloden.

The next day proved to be quite pleasant, although we were tired, we boarded our Hercules, on time. The only other passengers, were dressed in combat gear, and smothered in things that go bang. We attempted to hold a conversation with them, but got not a single response, they remained totally dead pan. I suspect they were special forces, with more on their minds than the quality of their next hotel rooms.

Upon arrival, at Dubai airbase, the British embassy, arranged to pick us up by taxi, and then took us to a very good hotel, in Dubai, where the embassy were picking up most of the cost. So we spent the rest of the day, sightseeing, eating and drinking. This was more like the trip we had planned.

The following morning, the embassy, once again sent chauffer driven cars, to collect us. These were large American, air conditioned vehicles, which was just as well, as we were heading across the desert, to meet 'HMS London', on the other side of the Persian Gulf, somewhere near Al-Fujairah, a distance of about 100Km.

We were eventually dropped, at a small village, where an Arab sat in a small hut, full of communications equipment. This was in contact with the ship, which was racing up the gulf to meet us. As the ship was about 4 hours away, we were once again obliged, to sit in a small café, eating and drinking. By the time the ship appeared on the horizon, we were not in any mood or condition, to start looking for problems once on board. The ship sent a 'Pas' boat to collect us, and we were on board, just in time for the evening meal, in the Wardroom. Even though we were in tropical temperatures, the mess informed us that, they always dressed for dinner, which meant a minimum of shirt and tie. It now turned out that every bunk on the ship was taken, as they had press, and other visitors on board. The total complement, was around 300 persons, on a ship that normally carried around 250. The ship agreed to set up camp beds for us, near the rear of the vessel, however as the 2 Mikes didn't get on, the senior one, asked for individual accommodation. This he later regretted, as the crew placed his bed in one of the machinery rooms, where the level of noise was deafening.

We then met in the wardroom, for dinner. It became clear that Mike M. had not taken the dress for dinner bit quite in the manner intended. He had on a smart shirt and tie, however from the waist down, it was shorts and flip-flops. The 2 Mikes, then spent most of the evening, arguing over R.N. tradition, and letting the side down, etc. So Trevor and I let them get on with it, and partook of lots of booze, at almost giveaway prices. R.N. wardroom food is generally O.K. till you get to the pudding, then they revert to appalling, 'Public school' food, like semolina, with a blob of jam in the middle.

The next day the job started in earnest, we tracked a number of targets, until we identified the problem, with the radar tracker. After resolving the problem, we the carried out 2, low level, confidence firings, of the missile system, and blew both targets out of the sky.

At the end of the day, we returned to the wardroom, where the assembled officers, congratulated us, and shook our hands etc. We were feeling pretty good! It is a tradition, that after a success, instead of the ship thanking the contractor, the contractors normally buy a few bottles of champagne, for the wardroom. I have never thought this fair, as only the officers benefit, not the rest of the crew. As a result, I stated that instead of champagne, I would buy, everyone on board a beer. This was so unusual, that the First Lt. had to go and ask the Captain. He came down to see me, and pointed out that there were over 300 people, on board. But once offered, it is difficult to go back, and anyway I thought I was spending Marconi's money. So everyone on board, had a beer on me, and we kept on meeting sailors, who congratulated us, on our efforts.

The ship was due to sail further up the Gulf, the next day, as the war was due to start, in 36 hours. As such the crew arranged a 'Pas' boat, to take us off, the next morning.

The next morning, I was walking along the passageway, past the wardroom, on may way to freedom, when a mess steward, jumped out in front of me. "Are you, the man, who fixed, the radar?" says he. Thinking he was also about to shake my hand, and being a modest type, I said "One of them, yes!"

"Well, you didn't do us any f-----g favours. We were going home, if you'd failed!" said he.

Just as we were leaving, the French admiral, was being piped on board. It always struck me as ironic for a French Admiral, as he was called 'Jon Bull'.

We were then un-ceremonially, dumped on the shore, by the 'Pas' boat, with no idea how to get home. 'This is the Royal Navy's way of saying 'thank you', now we no longer need you. If we had not been with a couple of R.N. officers, we would probably still be there! Eventually, they managed to get us to a military airbase, where a number of soldiers were thrown off their Hercules flight, to Riyadh, in order to accommodate us. We arrived in Riyadh just in time to board, one of the last flights out, before the war started. This was delayed for several hours, as just before take off, one of the passengers, who had raced across country, to catch the flight, had a heart attack, and died on the plane. Even at this stage, no one really expected the war to begin exactly on the deadline, and we were very surprised, on arrival back in the U.K. to find it was fully underway.

The next day I went into work, at Frimley, expecting, to receive general congratulations, only to find that no one would sign my expenses, as they would not sign for 300 cans of beer!

In the end I had to go to the unit Managing Director, who reluctantly agreed, that I probably, could not have drunk, 300 cans of beer in 3 days.

'Happy days'

Lord Harkness of Kilnsea.

In the year of our Lord, 2000, The then Labour government, came up with a ploy, to place more friends and sympathisers, into the House of Lords, under the guise of 'Peoples Peers'. The positions were open to all members of the public, and I like many others, and being rather naive, and believing the applications to be genuine, applied. At the time, I was not aware of the level of corruption, within politics, I spent months, along with friends and referees, preparing my application, but in the event not a 'single' member of the general public was selected.

Below is a copy of a letter I sent to the 'Sunday Times' after being turned down. (I don't know if it was published.)

Letters to the Editor,
Sunday Times

Cairnhill,
****
****
DG9 ***

30/04/01

PEOPLES PEERAGES

Dear Sir,

I was somewhat disappointed not to have been selected, for a peoples life peerage. However I find it very hard to understand the reasons given by Lord Stevenson for my rejection. Namely, that I would not feel comfortable in either ermine, or in debate.

I hope the following points, help illustrate my suitability for the Peerage;

1, I have the capability, to regularly imbibe, large quantities, of good quality claret.

2, It has been noted amongst my peers, that a capability exists, for generating large and regular expense claims.

3, Doing up my own shoelaces, is a little beyond me.

4, A reasonable proportion of the civilised world, has stood transfixed, by my ability to communicate, especially when assisted, by a quantity of vintage port.

I do however understand, that there are several impediments to my selection, which may be insurmountable, namely;

1, I appear to have served my country loyally, for 40 years, both as a member of Her Majesty's armed forces, and for 27 years as a civilian, in the Defence industry.

2, I have failed miserably, to kill or maim anything, either on the wing, pad, or hoof.

3, Normally, I can remember, what happened yesterday.

It is also with some apprehension, that I now feel, my family may have upset the balance, of the recent national census, due to our filling in the form, as Lord and Lady, in the firm belief, that my appointment, was a mere formality.

Yours faithfully,
David R. Harkness. (Life Peer failed)

(It now turns out, item 2 was prophetic!)

****Anyway I was so incensed, at being refused, that I did what everyone else does, I purchased a title. The main difference being, that I paid for my 'Feudal title' above board, rather than donating to a political party.

My title of 'Lord Harkness of Kilnsea', is for amusement, although, there are still the odd one or two, who touch their forelock. (I think they are taking the Mick.)

🐾

Being driven to drink.

I have always enjoyed a drink, and back in around 1988, I spent several months, working on a French missile range, in Bordeaux.

Well naturally, I took advantage of the large selection of Bordeaux wines and cognacs, and felt it my duty to fully test as many as possible. Needless to say, that as the trip came to an end I was not feeling too good. I was getting lots of pins and needles, in my arms, and generally felt under the weather. At the time I attributed this to the drink, but as it turned out a couple of years later, it was heart surgery that I really needed.

Anyway on return to my cottage in Wales, I decided to go and see the 'Quack'.

The doctor was a nice guy, who gave me a fairly thorough examination. He then gave me a long lecture on excessive drinking, told me to cut down on alcohol, and to stop drinking altogether for a few weeks. So I had several weeks, where all I drank was low alcohol, lager. (I find lager bad enough, with alcohol in, without it, it is purgatory.) This was and still is, the longest period I have ever gone without drink. The second longest period was when I had a triple, heart bypass, and was stuck in hospital, in Glasgow for 5 days.

The climax to this short tale, is that shortly after my visit to him, the doctor, who lectured me on drink, was banned from driving, for a year, after being caught, driving over the limit. "He spent a year visiting his patients, by being driven around by his wife."

Highly Confidential

Back in 1974, I was employed by the Marconi Co. carrying out Tracking Radar Trials in South West Scotland.

At the time, the transmitter for the radar was 'Secret', and involved employing at least 2 personnel as escort, when moving it around the country. We decided we required a replacement transmitter urgently, and contacted our base in Surrey, to get one to us. It was decided that the quickest means of getting the transmitter to us was to conduct a half way swap. The total journey, one way, was around 400miles, so the decision was made to exchange the item at 'Forton' services near Lancaster, on the M6. Two people would drive up to Forton with the transmitter, and two of us from site, would travel down to meet them, and collect it. The security guard, who had been delegated to escort the transmitter, rang me up, and asked a lot of pointless security questions, such as 'Our car registration, model, colour etc.' Then he gave me a code word to use when we exchanged the item. 'This all appeared very professional'. He the took both our names and gave me his name and his drivers.

So the next morning, off we start, to drive to 'Forton' a drive of around 4 hours. The planned changeover was for midday, after which we intended going for a relaxing pub lunch.

All went well, we arrived at 'Forton' in good time and sat around waiting for the arrival of the car from Surrey. This was in the days before mobile phones, so we had no contact with the other vehicle. 12-30pm went by, 1-00pm went by, 2-00pm went by, still no sign of the other car, which we presumed was stuck in traffic. By 3-00pm our patience was seriously depleted, and we rang our parent company in Surrey. This is what we were told;

The car from Surrey had got to about 20miles from 'Forton' when the security guard said to the driver, "What is it we are delivering?" and received the following reply, "I don't know, you're bringing it, aren't you?" Needless to say the 'Transmitter' was still sitting on a bench in Surrey.

'WORKING FOR A LIVING'

Back in 1971, I was still in the RAF, and started to rent a house in Hull, Yorkshire.

My wife and I, rented an end of terrace, 'Victorian' 4 bedroom house, from a Mrs. Norfolk. The house was moderately grand, and furnished in good Edwardian pieces, although, a bit old and faded. This was in the days before everyone, collected antiques, and there were lots of interesting items around, that Mrs. Norfolk, had collected, over many years. It turned out that she had a good eye for business. She owned several flats and houses, in Hull, along with a small Hotel. Subsequently we learnt that she was known in the area, as a pretty unforgiving 'Landlady', who would eject tenants at a moments notice.

She herself was quite a character, being about 4ft 6inches tall, aged around 50, and permanently wore a long mink coat, (I believe this was genuine), no matter what the weather.

Mrs Norfolk, ran the hotel, close to the centre of Hull. I visited the hotel on a couple of occasions, and found this also to be well furnished in 'Victorian' style. Her husband drove a privately owned Taxi, as his contribution, and all other members of the family were gainfully employed, as I subsequently found.

Mrs Norfolk's, children lived in the house next door to us, and were a boy and a girl, both aged about 30.

The particular area of Hull, in which we resided, was generally middle class, and had a good private school close by. However it was impossible to leave anything lying about. I was working on my car one day, and drove around the block, in order to test the vehicle. I must have been gone no more than 5 minutes, when on my return, I found all of my tools had been stolen. On another occasion, all the pot plants were stolen out of our porch.

We had a small party, for a few friends, and when the first of them arrived, we went to the pub, leaving a note on the door saying 'Party here', so that late arrivals would know the venue was correct.

Upon our return from the pub, we were met by a house, jammed to the gills with party goers, we had never met. The wife went to bed in hysterics, but I had a most enjoyable night! Some of the uninvited guests, turned out to be great entertainers, and they had brought along a lot of booze.

The above is just to give a feel for the area, before I describe the 2 children.

I was a SNCO at the time, and on returning home, one day, I lost my RAF 'beret'. I could not find it, anywhere, and replaced it with a new one. Several months after losing the beret, I glanced out of the window, and noticed Mrs. Norfolk's son, marching up and down the street, wearing my 'beret', and with a broom handle over his shoulder. He was doing a pretty good impression of a 'goose step' and saluting, all and sundry, as he passed.

We also noticed, that the daughter, only appeared in the evenings, she was always dressed up, had lots of make-up on, and had several black patches, stuck on her face.

We subsequently found, she was a working girl, who operated from her mothers hotel, and her brother and father, acted as the pimps, and procured the clients. 'A real family business.' Most of the clients were obtained by the father, who suggested the hotel and other services, to any male, he picked up in his taxi.

'However, the whole operation took a bit of a tumble, when the 'police' stopped his taxi, in the early hours of the morning, and he fell out at their feet, in an alcoholic stupor.'

I don't know how business was afterwards!

🐾

The Big Hard Farmer.

I have a farmer friend, in Cumbria, who won't mind me telling this very short tale.

Peter, is not like most farmers, (other than being rude to everyone he meets), in that he does not possess a gun, and is very kind to his animals. He will constantly, call in the vet, at great expense, even though, he knows there is almost no chance of an animal surviving. If an animal eventually needs destroying, he either calls in the vet, to put it down, or gets a friend to shoot it, while he is not looking.

One day he was cleaning out his barn, after the beasts, had gone out to pasture, only to find, a nest of baby bunnies, among the old straw. So being the hard man he is, he scooped the baby rabbits up, and placed them in a bucket lined with fresh straw. He then continued with his cleaning of the barn. Upon completion, Peter, then carefully made a new nest for the bunnies, and placed them back, exactly as found.

No doubt, they re-paid his kindness, by prospering, and subsequently, eating all his garden vegetables.

"Mike and the Casino girl"

Mike is his real name and I know he will be quite proud to feature in this little tale. We have been good friends for many years, and worked together on Naval missile radars until his retirement. Mike was ex Navy and typical of many a naval Chief petty officer, not unintelligent when sober, but sometimes these periods were few and far between. At the time of this incident he was living in a rented flat in Southsea, with a Glaswegian girl, Liz, who he had met in a Glasgow pub by the expedient of accidentally throwing his beer over her. At the time of this tale, he had been with Liz for about 3 years, and the occasional argument had turned into a regular event.

Mike was now about 58 years of age, and an inveterate gambler. He would bet on almost anything, however he never lost when you spoke to him, either that or he only mentioned the wins.

Liz had just been re-united, with her father, who had previously done a runner when she was just a kid. She had found him after months of investigation, and he had decided he loved his daughter after all. So she was away in Brighton for a few days with daddy, leaving Mike at a bit of a loose end. Well being a bit of a social animal with no love of his own company, Mike decided to pop into his local pub in Southsea, for a couple of pints. So a couple of pints and several dark rums later, the urge was on him to head into Portsmouth, where he once again popped into a pub with which he was regularly conversant. Having had a pleasant evening and full of the joys of life, he was somewhat disappointed when the pub landlord decided it was time he went home, and ejected him onto the lonely streets of the town.

Well, what is a lonely chap to do after midnight, but wander around a bit and find a touch of entertainment. Suddenly Mike was confronted by the glorious flashing lights of the Casino, and felt that tonight his luck must be in. Also he had a system for roulette, which I believe consisted of sticking all your money on red and closing your eyes. Today, (by now tomorrow), the system genuinely appeared to be working, and after about an hour the boy was a thousand pounds up, which along with his original stake, meant he had around £1200 in chips. 'Common sense' a rare commodity with Mike, took hold and he decided to cash in his chips and call it a night. Now Mike is about five foot four, showing signs of good living and is not the prettiest guy around, so this next event may have given him some room for doubt, if it hadn't been for the contents of around a bottle of rum, floating around inside him. Just as he was leaving the Casino, a very tall, attractive girl, came up to him and told him she fancied him. Not being shy, he then invited her to join him for a drink, at the Casino bar. Several drinks later, she agreed to accompany him back to his flat.

Upon arrival at the flat, Mike removed the £1200 from his pocket, and placed it in the dressing table drawer, after which they immediately embraced, and had just started to undress when Mike felt an urgency to use the toilet, so he quickly excused himself and vanished to relieve his bladder. Upon returning 5 minutes later, he was a little surprised to find the front door open, and no sign of his date! She had evidently left in something of a hurry, as her shoes and stockings were still scattered around the floor. Being a pretty bright sort of guy, after about 5 minutes, he decided he better check his winnings, and lo and behold, where once £1200 had resided, there was now just an empty space.

So extremely incensed, Mike picked up the phone and dialled 999, he then asked to be put through to the police, who enquired as to his emergency. "A bleeding hooker has just lifted £1200 off me" he said, at which point he was sure the cop on the other end tittered with laughter, and told him they didn't consider it an emergency! "Well I do" says Mike. "In that case you had better come into the station tomorrow, and we'll take a statement" was the reply.

So the following morning, Mike pops into the local police station, carrying the girls shoes and stockings. (She must have been tough, because not only was it mid winter, but it had been raining heavily, and she was running in bare feet!). From what he told me, the police didn't seem to take his predicament very seriously, as he said they kept grinning while taking his statement.

Subsequently after getting back home, he spent the next 2 weeks worrying, in case the police actually caught his absent friend, and turned up at the flat, reciting the evenings events while Liz was in, which would have greatly increased his troubles. But as you might expect, the police found nothing, and I expect the girl did not bother to try and claim her shoes, after all, she had plenty of cash for many a pair!

'Has Mike learnt anything from this? Not likely."

"Under cover in Switzerland"

Back in the mid 1970's, while working in Switzerland, we were carrying out radar trials way up in the mountainous regions. There were around 10 of us in the team, composed of members of the British Aircraft Corporation, Marconi and Decca. We were staying in a rather pleasant, chalet type hotel, where we had been resident for several weeks. At the time a long term friend of mine, Colin, (Known universally as 'Coggie'), was part of the team.

We had just finished a successful series of trials, and had been invited out to dinner that night by our Swiss hosts, in order to celebrate.

We all had an exceptionally enjoyable evening, and started back to the hotel in the early hours of the following morning. I might say it was also winter, and snowing heavily, but reinforced by alcohol and good humour, we arrived back at the hotel, only to find the doors locked and barred, and no way in. The owners of the establishment lived in a separate bungalow, about 100 yards away from the main hotel. Venturing there we found everything in darkness and so banged very loudly on the bungalow front door, until a very, very grumpy, and ill tempered owner eventually appeared in pyjamas. He then had to get dressed and walk with us over to the hotel, in order to let us all in.

After opening up the hotel, he gave a us a grumpy goodnight, and vanished back to his house and bed. So in we all pop and everyone heads for their rooms, when I get to mine I realise I have not got the bedroom door key. No problem, I'm thinking, I left the key on the hook in the dining room, and so I head downstairs to collect it. 'This is where it all goes wrong.' The dining room door is also locked! (The Swiss take security very seriously). Well I could see my key, through the glass door but had no way of getting to it, other than venturing out into the snow again, and getting an already fed up owner, once again out of bed. As this option did not appear very appealing, I decided I would sleep in the corridor, however it was quite cold and I knocked on 'Coggies' bedroom door, in order to borrow a blanket. "Don't be a fool" he says, "You can share my bed, as long as you don't snore". So in we both get, with our underclothes on, and a sheet between us. Having had plenty to drink, in no time at all we are both sound asleep!

The next thing we hear is the bedroom door opening followed by a cheery "Gutten Morgan" as the maid arrived with the morning tea. Suddenly both of us sat up in bed at the same time. The maid gave a sudden 'squeak' and vanished back out of the door, only to return 5 minutes later with 2 cups of tea. (Very professional). Having then washed and dressed, I headed downstairs to collect my key from the dining room. The usual, early morning chattering could be heard from the other guests, as I approached. As I entered the room, and reached up for my key, a sudden silence descended. (So word had travelled fast). Subsequently, on leaving the dining room, the noise level again increased! It was just as well our stay in that particular hotel, was coming to an end.

"They probably thought 'Coggie' and I had attended an English 'Public school'.

"The Disco"

Back in around 1980, I had a good friend John, who was around 50 years of age, and looked even older due to totally white hair. In spite of his age he was a great 'pop' music fan, who collected a lot of 45 rpm records.

One day while chatting, he disclosed to me that his long held ambition was to run a 'Disco,' however he had no way of financing it. So after a chat, it was agreed that we would become partners in the entertainment business. I would design and build the 'Disco' and acquire a van, and then John would run the show. The theory being that we would then share the vast profits!

After around 3 months things were more or less up and running. The Disco was operational, with lots of lights and speakers, and I had obtained an old but useable Ford Transit van, in order to move everything around. We named the Disco 'Reflections' as we had employed a large number of mirrors.

Our first couple of 'gigs' went quite well. These were small events in local bars. Then we obtained our first major job, supplying the music, at a large wedding reception. Initially everything went well, the venue being a large ballroom in a hotel. It was late summer and the evening was very hot, especially in the ballroom which was full of guests.

I was sat at home, watching T.V. which I remember very well, as 'Bucks Fizz' had just won the 'European song contest,' when the phone rang. A very agitated John, was on the other end. "The Disco has blown-up" says he. "Get here and fix it quick, as the crowd are getting mutinous". So I drive out 5 miles, and meet him in the hotel, where the guests were looking for blood, as the reception was only half over.

Initial inspection of the kit was not good. There were 2 power amplifiers, to supply the left and right speaker banks. These were mounted in wooden cases, which I had build without any form of cooling! Initially the left hand amplifier failed, due to overheating. This meant the volume now dropped as only one bank of speakers, remained working. John then being a true professional, who's only requirement was that the show must go on, turned up the volume on the right hand bank to maximum, to compensate.

Needless to say, shortly afterwards, the right hand bank also failed, leaving the room in total silence. 'Other than the mumbling of the crowd'.

So much power had been fed through the right hand amplifier, that it had melted both the cable and the speaker coils, before finally giving up the ghost.

John and I, made a cowardly, and very rapid departure, mumbling something about, see you soon! Before the crowd got to us. 'We never had the nerve to send a bill'

Subsequently, after a few modifications, the 'Disco' did fairly well. John made money, and I nearly covered my costs.

🐾

"A NEW COCKTAIL"

Around the same time as the Disco, I was working on the range at Portpatrick. We had a range vessel, the 'Aquilla Maris'. 'Pete' was the skipper, and very competent.

On this particular day, the weather was hot and calm, the boat a converted ex RAF Air/Sea rescue launch had been at sea for several hours. Pete had manipulated the area approaching the harbour at Portpatrick on very many occasions, without incident, even though the approach was very rocky.

Suddenly, just around lunchtime, a radio message was received at the range, implying the Aquilla Maris had gone aground while heading back in.

Anyway it was a glorious day, and I decided to walk down the cliff path to the 'Crown Hotel' for lunch, as I did most days. The walk was no more than 10 minutes, so I arrived in the bar of the 'Crown' not more than 15 minutes after receiving the radio call.

Upon arrival I was greeted by the barman 'Alan', who immediately asked me if I had tried their latest cocktail. "What cocktail" says I.

"Aquilla on the rocks" says Alan

At the time the Landlady of the 'Crown Hotel' was called 'Molly', she asked my advice one lunchtime, on a large ex railway station clock, she had just purchased for the hotel bar. Upon inspection, it was clear that the clock was just a repeater, that would have operated from a master clock, somewhere within the station. Not wishing to tell her she had been cheated by the dealer, I foolishly offered to make her a master clock, in order to run it.

So I purchased a large number of electronic parts. (at the time about £20, but this was around 1980, so not an insignificant amount), and set to work building the clock in my spare time. It took me around a week to complete the job, and installing it.

Upon completion, the clock worked well, and kept good time.

I decided I wouldn't charge for any of my time, but would ask just for the cost of the parts.

So into the bar I go, and ask Molly if she is happy with the clock!

"It's very good, how much do I owe you?" she says.

I was about to say; "That's all right, but would you pay £20 for the parts".

What I actually said was; "That's all right", and before I could add anything, she said. "Thank you Dave, you're very kind, have a 'pint' on the house.

'At least, with hand on heart, I can now say;

"I'm Dave Harkness, Clockmaker to the Crown"

🐾

'And Finally'

"A bit more on Freddie and his friends."

I have just retired, at the end of September 2009, at the age of 66 years, and feel about 40.

Retirement means I have stopped commuting constantly 200 miles each way, from Barrow-in Furness, where I have been employed for the last 2 years. For the last 18 months, 'Lusso' our 6 year old, Labrador cross, has been my constant companion and friend. He loved the life, and was well known, in several pubs in the area. We had a daily routine, where 'Lusso' and I drove 12 miles from the caravan site, to 'Barrow' where the warships on which I worked, were moored. The first thing we did was to go for a walk along the quay side, throwing a few balls, as we went! 'Lusso' is brilliant and quick at catching them, and then he would have to be lifted into the back of the car, 'a hangover from 'Bertie'. I would then go to work for an hour or so, and then we would go to 'Morrisons' supermarket, for breakfast. On returning, we would have another short walk, and then I would return to work until lunchtime. For lunch we visited a different Inn each day. We only used pubs where 'Lusso' was welcome, and he had lots of friends, to spoil him. Then we would head for the beach, where another walk ensued. Usually the afternoon at work was divided up by another short walk, and then we drove back to the caravan site. Upon arrival back on the site, most evening were spent conducting a 2 mile walk, with Tracey, the site owner, and her dog 'Midge'. If the evenings were pleasant, 'Lusso' and I would visit the pub for a quick pint, and then head back to the site. Subsequently, I would sit outside my caravan, and throw ball after ball for 'Lusso' to catch.

So you can see he was quite fond of 'Barrow', and still gives the impression of being ready to go back at any time. However all good things come to an end eventually, and he will have to get used to retirement, and with putting up with his 'friend?' and companion 'Freddie'. 'Freddie' wishes to be 'Lusso's' friend but it isn't reciprocal.

'Lusso' in 'Barrow (Ball in mouth)   (Frigates in the background)

Freddie's idea of fun is to jump in front of Lusso, just as he is trying to catch his ball. This does nothing to improve Lusso's love of him, and usually ends in grumps and growls. He also likes to try and steal Lusso's ball from out of his mouth, usually resulting in Lusso being covered in 'Droolies,' something else he hates. The 'Ball' is Lusso's greatest possession, and he will often lie with it in his mouth all evening, just to prevent it falling into the wrong hands.

However 'Finley' the cat is much more amenable to Freddie's attention, and will often come down from it's favourite sleeping spot on the mantelpiece, just to play with him. He is now 13 stone and still thinks he is the same size as the cat. His paws are bigger than the cats head, yet sometimes he gives the cat a friendly paw, sending it flying. The cat doesn't seem to care, unless he accidentally lies on it, and even then they still remain friends. Freddie does occasionally manage to get the entire cats head in his mouth, never doing it any harm, other than covering it in so much slaver, that the cat takes hours to clean itself. The only thing he does maliciously, is to sit with his bum firmly against the cat door, preventing the cats entry/exit. This does annoy 'Finley' who spits at him with no visible effect.

I now have 2 permanent shadows, as everywhere I go, Lusso and Freddie are there. Lusso normally with his ball in his mouth.

I have only been retired 1 month and it is true what everyone says! "How did I have time to go to work."

To be continued?

About the Author.

David Harkness was born in Leeds, Yorkshire, in 1943. He was brought up in Leeds and mainly York and was educated very badly, in the early post war, secondary school system. As a schoolboy, he was interested in Amateur radio and anything else electrical, often going to auction sales and buying up old televisions and radios, to experiment with. After attending Technical college in Bishop Auckland, his first job was as an apprentice plater, until he joined the RAF at age17, where his first involvement with 'Radar' occurred. In 1973 he joined the 'Marconi' company and spent the next 36 years in Radar development and trials.

He has finally retired to south west Scotland, where he lives with his wife 'Dottie', two dogs, a cat, an old stationary, steam, mill engine and a 1979 Rolls car, that costs far more to keep on the road than it is ever worth.